Goodbye, Sammartino

Michael Herlihy

Michael Herlihy

Copyright © 2018 Michael Herlihy

All rights reserved.

ISBN:099955414X
ISBN-13:978-0-9995541-4-2

DEDICATION

For my sons

Michael Herlihy

ACKNOWLEDGMENTS

Cover Photo "Creative Commons Harvard Stadium" by Ted Eytan
is licensed under CC BY 2.0

Chapter One

He dragged his left leg as though he was pulling the past behind him. His face was obscured because his long black hair draped over his eyes like a curtain and I wondered how he ever knew where he was going. He could have passed for a freshman because he was so short and slight, nothing like someone who was supposed to be a senior. Just like every time I saw him, I thought about how reckless and irresponsible he'd been.

I was waiting for Jack on our way out to the locker room for baseball practice. Where Bernie Kimball was going was anyone's guess.

Bernie had limped ever since the accident. He and another kid had driven home after a night of partying in the woods with the freaks behind the high school, if you call smoking a ton of pot and drinking beer in the dark partying. He plowed his '65 Impala into a maple tree at the fork in Independence Road. There were no skid marks or any signs that he had tried to turn left or right because he probably had been so high that he never noticed the split.

The Chevy's front end wrapped around the tree like metal arms and the windshield crumpled into hundreds of shards where his friend's head went through on the passenger's side. The collision pushed the steering column into the car and pinned Bernie to the driver's seat, breaking most of his lower ribcage and crushing his left hip socket. Somehow the kid in the passenger's seat survived and was going to graduate in a couple of months. Bernie, though, was hospitalized for a long time and missed most of the last school year. He was repeating the eleventh grade because he had so much class time to make up.

I knew all the details. Everyone did. It had been a Monday night and Bernie had been driving without a license. His license had been suspended for driving under the influence. A Monday night. With school the next day.

Bernie saw me and stopped. He was with one of his freak friends. The freaks are the drug users at school, or so everyone says. They're equal parts long hair and indifference. Bernie, I assumed, was headed for the woods at the edge of school grounds, beyond the baseball field.

Bernie and his friend waited, just to kill time until I left, and then they disappeared into a school entrance. The freaks stay clear of the jocks in school. I guess he figured I was like the other jocks who gave the freaks a hard time. I didn't care what Bernie did. He left me alone and that was fine with me.

Coach Adams came out of the locker room and was walking toward me. He was lugging an equipment bag. "Aiden, how ya doin'?"

"Coach."

"See you at practice." He lumbered past me.

A couple of minutes later, I was outside with Jack, my closest friend since forever, for practice. I stared out at the parking lot full of cars belonging to teachers, visitors and students. Mr. Hentz, one of my favorite teachers at Kennedy because he treats me as though he cares as much about me as about my grades, was leaving. I could imagine him as a sea captain sailing off New Bedford, searching for whales. I could see him at the bow, gripping the wheel, and calling out orders. He's over six feet tall with a deep, resonant voice that sounds like it comes out of a barrel. And he wears suits.

The sky outside was cloudless and lake blue. Baseball practice would be good with this kind of weather. Yesterday we practiced in a steady drizzle while someone played their car radio just beyond left field. They just sat there listening to music. There's never a bad time to be on a baseball field, but it got old wiping mud off the ball every time I got it. Late April rain is way more tolerable than March's, which makes me shiver and hope I don't catch the ball in the palm of my glove and get a hand sting that will last for the rest of practice.

Coach Adams played baseball and football at Howard and is one of the few black people in our town. He coaches varsity football, too, and thinks weather should have no effect on practice, except that in football you can slog through rain and snow but baseball takes more finesse. If the weather is too cold or wet, it messes up the game because you can't grip the ball right or throw it well. Of course, none of us say anything because he's the coach and he's the one who attended college on a scholarship, so he obviously knows more than us.

Mr. Hentz saw me and waved. Another thing I like about Mr. Hentz is that he doesn't get bent out of shape if your mind wanders in class. He doesn't act like Algebra class is supposed to be the same as hanging out with one of the Beatles. I've had teachers who almost blow a gasket if you don't act like they're the most interesting person in the world and more beautiful or handsome than a movie star.

Chapter Two

When I got home after practice, my father's garment bag was propped next to the front door in the hallway. My dad was sitting in an easy chair in the living room under a portrait of my grandparents, the one next to a photograph of my brother, Sean, graduating from Marine Corps boot camp at Parris Island. My dad had his legal briefcase open on his lap and he was going through some papers. My mother was still at work. She had gone back to work once I got to high school. Since Eileen was closer to graduating, my mom had said she wanted to make more money for her college. I also think that with us getting older, she was preparing for when we wouldn't be around the house.

He was going to New York for just a couple of days to meet with a client of his firm, but I felt sad anyway.

My Aunt Lindy came into the room, wiping her hands on a kitchen towel. "There's a taxi in the driveway." She had recently moved in with us.

My aunt was my father's eldest sister and was nearly a generation older than him. She had sprays of curly salt and pepper hair that was in perpetual need of a brush and had a solid, robust shape that made her legs seem like roots to the earth. Her eyeglasses were about fifteen years out of date, but they fit her perfectly. I could not have imagined her wearing any other kind of glasses.

I glanced out the living room window and saw a canary yellow cab idling. It was a taxi for a company owned by the family of a kid I went to school with. The forsythias at the edge of the driveway matched the color of the cab, except where they were starting to turn green.

My father wasn't real demonstrative, but he squeezed the back of my neck when he stood up. He had been doing more of that stuff recently. I think it's my mother's influence.

"I'll call when I get to New York." He looked at my aunt. "Give my love to Eileen and let her know I'll call."

My sister was still at high school, rehearsing with the cast for the spring play. She was providing musical accompaniment on the piano. My dad knew better than to tell me to send Eileen his love. It would sound too goofy coming from me and she'd probably think I was being sarcastic, anyway.

"The meter's running," my aunt said.

"It's okay, Lindy. It's not like when we were kids."

I picked up my dad's garment bag, opened the front door, and carried his stuff out to the cab. The driver, a big guy with a pot belly, got out, opened the trunk, and put the bag inside it. He slammed the trunk shut. I said goodbye to my dad and stepped back onto the lawn.

My aunt joined me as my dad got into the back seat of the taxi. She put her arm around my shoulders the way my mother might have done. Her arm felt as warm as the sun's rays.

We waved goodbye as the taxi backed out of the driveway. The taxi driver had to take it slowly because there is a huge oak tree at the end of the driveway that blocks your view and makes it hard to turn. My sister crushed the right front fender a while back when she first had her learner's permit because she cut the turn too sharp. Of course, she said it was the tree's fault for being too big.

Aunt Lindy kept her arm around my shoulders. "He'll be back in a couple of days," she said, as though she could sense what I was thinking.

My aunt and I walked back into the house. I closed the front door behind us and the door knob squeaked as I turned it and the latch clicked into place. My aunt went to the pantry next to the kitchen where we stored canned and boxed foods. Next, she opened the refrigerator and spent a minute or two taking inventory.

"Do you want to come to the market with me?" she said.

I thought it over. Aunt Lindy was one person you could be honest with and she'd accept your point of view, without trying to make you into a different person or trying to change your mind. "I was hoping to throw against the garage."

"I won't be long anyway."

I threw a tennis ball against the garage most days, to strengthen my arm and sharpen my fielding. My brother had nailed a plywood board over the back window when he was playing varsity baseball so that he could throw every day. I was just following in his footsteps, figuring it was just something you did. It had worked. My arm was so strong that even as a freshman on varsity, I had one of the strongest throwing arms.

My father had cleared out scrub pines to make enough room for a sixty and a half foot pitching lane for Sean. Then he installed a pitching rubber. One of the good things about being a younger brother is you benefit from things done before you, like a pitching lane in the backyard.

My aunt got her purse and a silk kerchief that she wrapped around her head. She slipped on a thin coat that she had been wearing for years. My dad once tried to buy her a new one, but she wouldn't have it.

"It's such a nice day that I'll walk," she said.

"You know what, Aunt Lindy? I'll go with you."

I was glad we were walking because the other drivers would be spared her notoriously bad driving. She did so many things well, like sing and play the piano and make people around her feel wonderful, but she must have been absent the day they were handing out driving skills.

We set off for the A&P on foot, which was less than a quarter mile at most from where we lived. Our town is one of those suburbs of Boston that was founded before the American Revolution and has a common and old parkland that the citizens have made it a point to preserve. It seems like such a quiet place where nothing ever happens.

We went through the aisles of the grocery store, picking out her favorite things, TableTalk pies, potato chips, and a bag of hard peppermint candies. Somehow a head of lettuce slipped in to our cart. We checked out and walked home.

I threw against the garage when we got back, aiming each throw at the square my brother had painted in the middle of the plywood for a target. Baseball always made me feel better. You could control at least some of what happened in a game. Life, not so much.

I threw for about fifteen minutes and went back inside. Aunt Lindy had the kettle boiling on the stovetop to the sink.

"I'm going to have some tea. Would you like a snack?" She went to the sink, turned on the faucet, and filled a glass of water. "What's for supper?" she said.

My aunt was also absent the day they passed out cooking skills.

"Dad said we could order something or go out since Mom is working late."

"That's lovely."

Everything was lovely to Aunt Lindy.

She went to the kitchen table and glanced at the headlines of the *Boston Globe*. "People have to wait so long for gas. It reminds me of World War Two when we had to watch our use of everything."

"We talked about the oil embargo in class the other day."

The kettle whistled. I turned the flame off. I poured the boiling water over a tea bag in a Boston College mug. I brought the tea to my aunt, who was sitting and reading the paper.

"Would you bring the pie, dearie?"

I got the pie from the counter and placed it, and a plate and knife, in front of her. She opened the box, cut herself a piece, and laid it on the plate. "Would you like some, too?"

"No, thanks. I'll wait for dinner." I wanted some, but it was the middle of baseball season and I was training. Being the only freshman on varsity, I had to get every edge to improve my playing chances.

"What will we have for supper?"

"We don't have to go out. I can make hot dogs and beans or something."

"Lovely."

I watched her eat a forkful of pie. "I remember when we'd visit Grandma and you'd always make her tea and make sure she had a blanket on her lap," I said.

My grandmother had spent her last years in a wheelchair in the house my father's family grew up in. Aunt Lindy had taken care of her and had never married. We visited her and my grandmother every Sunday and my father would stop at a lake on the way home and let us feed the ducks with stale bread. I really miss those days.

Chapter Three

Eileen came home as I was setting the table. She put her books on the spot where I was about to put a plate.

"How was school, dearie?"

"It was fine, Aunt Lindy." She went to my aunt and kissed her on the cheek. "Except for Robert Erskine."

"Who's Robert Erskine?"

"The lead in the school play and he's impossible."

"Speaking of impossible," I said. "Can you move your stuff off the table?"

Eileen sighed dramatically.

"Your father will be back before you know it," my aunt said. "He sends his love."

Eileen forgot about her issues with Robert Erskine's personality for a moment. She gathered her books and took them away from the table.

The three of us sat down for dinner. I said grace. "Bless us, oh Lord, and these thy gifts, which we are about to receive from thy bounty through Christ our Lord. Amen."

We all blessed ourselves and dug in.

"So what's wrong with this boy?" my aunt said.

"He thinks he's God's gift."

"He doesn't realize you are?" I said. I smiled angelically at Eileen.

Eileen ignored me. "He thinks because he can sing that he's the best thing in the play."

We usually never had discussions like this at dinner. I guess it was because my aunt was here and my parents were not.

"Did he say that?" my aunt said.

"No, but you can tell."

"You can just tell what?"

I observed my sister and aunt talking. Sometimes I wondered if my aunt was sharper than she let on. I got the sense that she was leading Eileen with her questions. But maybe she wasn't.

"What?" Eileen said.

"You can tell what?" my aunt said. "That he sings well or he's conceited."

Eileen was confused for a moment. "Both."

I wished my brother Sean was still living with us, so that we could talk about wrestling or baseball. When I was little, I had thought he was going to be around forever. He left for the Marines when I was in junior high and I had assumed he would return and things would go back to the way they'd always been.

I used to go to the high school track with him and sit in the bleachers and watch him run laps when he was preparing for boot camp.

After coming home from Vietnam, he wasn't the same. He barely got an honorable discharge after going AWOL from Camp Pendleton. Since his discharge, we haven't seen much of him. He may be living in Boston somewhere or New York City. Any place is possible. He might be hitching rides in Nebraska, for all we know. It had been almost two years since any of us had seen or heard from him. It's strange how someone can be so important to you and then, all of a sudden, it's as though they no longer exist, even if they haven't died.

"Aiden?" my sister said loudly. "I've been trying to get your attention."

"I wasn't listening."

"No kidding.

"Is everything all right, dearie?" My aunt's voice was soothing, like ointment rubbed on a burn.

"Can I go outside and throw for a while?" I said. "I'm not very hungry."

"What about the dishes?" Eileen said. You'd have thought I had just shorted her change at the store.

My aunt wrinkled her forehead. Whatever she was thinking, I never felt judged by her. She was too big-hearted. "Go ahead, dearie."

"Thanks, Aunt Lindy." I got up and did something I'd never done before. I put my arm around her shoulders. She reached up from where she was sitting and held my arm in both her hands. "I'll do the dishes when I come in."

I left the kitchen, picked up a tennis ball and my glove, and went to the back yard. I threw against the garage, pretending to be Jim Lonborg in the '67 Series, but I kept wondering why Sean left. He was becoming more and more a memory than a brother.

Chapter Four

The day my father returned from New York we were at the kitchen sink doing the dishes after supper. My aunt was in the den watching television because my dad had told her we'd clean up, even though she offered to do them. My dad and my aunt have a special bond. You can just feel it and sense it when you're around them. He'd do anything for her.

"Do you like having Aunt Lindy live with us?" he said.

"Yeah. I think it's great. I feel good when she's around."

"She's always been like that. Not everyone has that effect on people, but your aunt does."

"She wants to get fabric tomorrow to make a throw," my father said. "Do you want to go with her?"

"Sure, Dad."

It would be Saturday. I was hoping we could leave after noon, so that I could watch wrestling. Wrestling came on at eleven on Saturday morning and was as reliable as the sunrise and had been the one time during the week when Sean and I used to sit down together. I kept watching it every Saturday, even though it was obvious to me it was fake. I mean, how many people get up after being body slammed by a three-hundred pound brute? It's no fun poking fun at how fake it is when you're watching it alone. At least with Sean, we could joke about it. I guess I kept tuning it in sort of in memory of him, but it had started to feel rote.

"Are you ready to go?" It was quarter to noon on Saturday and my aunt had come into the den where I had tuned in wrestling.

"Sure, Aunt Lindy," I said, trying to suppress my disappointment.

Bruno Sammartino hadn't come on for the main match. Bruno was the champ and was never on television and I didn't want to miss him. In certain circles, he occupied a place something like that of Bobby Orr.

You had to go to the Garden for one of the monthly matches to see Bruno, because the WWWF, the World Wide Wrestling Federation, kept him off TV. It's "world wide" because they want you to think that the wrestlers come from the four corners of the earth, when most of them probably grew up around Schenectady.

Pro wrestling really knows how to lead you on.

My aunt noticed. "What's the matter, dearie?"

"Nothing. I was just hoping to watch the next match."

"You can do that. I'm in no hurry."

My aunt just became the coolest adult on the planet, if she hadn't been already.

The villain facing Bruno brought a foreign object into the ring that everyone, except the referee, saw. He jabbed Bruno a couple times with it and put it under his arm when the ref tried to inspect him. The crowd was screaming for the ref to check the guy's armpit, but I guess the ref was deaf, because, of course, he didn't. When the ref wasn't looking, the villain took out the foreign object, but Bruno was ready, grabbed it, and tossed it in the crowd, which is pretty nasty when you think that it was just in the guy's armpit.

Then Bruno put the guy in a backbreaker and he submitted. Order had been restored in the world. Aunt Lindy sat next to me through the whole match. It wasn't nearly the same as watching it with Sean, but I appreciated her pinch-hitting, so to speak. But a pinch hitter still isn't a starter.

I turned the set off at the end of the broadcast and we walked out to the driveway. My aunt successfully backed the car out of the driveway and we got to the town line without incident.

Chapter Five

My aunt merged our Plymouth onto the two-lane state highway that led north from our town toward New Hampshire. She swerved onto the road like she'd hit a patch of ice, except the road was clear and dry.

I had tried to convince her to take the back roads. "It will be more scenic, Aunt Lindy." But she thought the highway would be faster.

It amazed me that she had lived to retirement age, the way she drove, but she had mainly relied on the public transportation near her apartment.

A car behind us in the right lane leaned on the horn. I turned around and the car was practically in the back seat. You'd have thought we had the guy's wallet.

"Why does he keep beeping?"

"I think he wants you to go faster than thirty miles per hour."

The driver swung around us into the passing lane. He pulled next to us and gave us the finger. My aunt didn't see it because she was staring straight ahead and because she has no peripheral vision.

"You better speed up," I said. I didn't know which was scarier, Aunt Lindy crawling on a state highway or Aunt Lindy driving faster on a state highway.

I realized that I had been clutching the side of my seat. If my grip had been any harder, I might have ripped off a chunk of vinyl.

We stayed in the right lane and I watched the pine trees blur together in the green median separating the north and south routes of the highway. We came to our exit, which was a connecting ramp that led down to one of the cities that grew up in this part of Massachusetts during the Industrial Revolution. The streets became constricted and narrow, with cars parked on both sides, and there were double-decker apartment buildings where women in housecoats sat on the stoops.

I had heard from the townies at school that Hell's Angels had a presence here. I wasn't sure whether to believe them, but they were the kids in black leather jackets who drove muscle cars and who started shaving in fifth grade. I figured that if anyone knew about this stuff, it was the townies.

The city seemed decayed to me compared to the trees and parks and houses where we lived. Here, the buildings were crushed together, the parks were asphalt basketball courts, and factory smoke clouded the sky.

I didn't recognize anything, even though I had been here before with my dad and brother for a Gold Gloves tournament. It had been at night and I didn't know what part of the city we were in or if we were near the arena.

I was reading the handwritten directions my father had given me. "Turn right here, Aunt Lindy."

She jerked the wheel and I slammed into the passenger's door. "You can take it a little slower," I said.

At the next intersection, she drove through without stopping.

"You just ran a stop sign." I looked around to see if there was a police car following us.

"What stop sign?"

We found the fabric store, a storefront with a big plate glass window and a few parking spaces in front of it. My aunt pulled our Plymouth into a slot, more or less. The other spaces were empty and it was probably not a big deal that we had taken up two.

We got out and I held the door to the store open for her. The smell of wool and cotton inside reminded me of my mother and the scent of laundry when she brought clothes to my room.

A young woman with raven-black hair met us at the counter. She waited as my aunt dug through her handbag for a list. My aunt found the list and showed it to the woman. She directed us to the rear of the store and we searched through fabric rolls that were big enough to be carpeting.

My aunt found beige fabric that felt like flannel and asked an older woman who spoke with an Italian accent to cut a piece for her. Then my aunt found a roll of string that was potato brown and almost as thick as yarn.

We took everything to the cash register and paid for the materials, which the raven-haired woman put in a white plastic bag, and we went to the car.

"I'd like some lunch," my aunt said after she had put the bag inside the car. "Let's go there." She pointed to a small pizza shop across the street.

A bald man with a fringe of hair above his ears was leaning against the door jamb, trying to hold himself or the building up. He was wearing a smeared white apron and smoking a cigarette.

We left the car at the fabric store lot and walked across the street. We got to the pizza shop and the man nodded wordlessly at us. He dropped his cigarette to the sidewalk and ground it into the pavement and seemed more annoyed than happy that we were there. Hardly the welcome wagon.

He followed us into the shop and went behind the counter. A schedule for the local high school football team that was two years out of date hung on the wall behind him, under the menu board and next to a restroom sign of a man and a woman.

I ordered a meatball grinder and a Coke. Aunt Lindy asked for a slice of cheese pizza and tea.

The man took a silver pan out of the refrigerator and scooped three meatballs onto a submarine roll. He ladled tomato sauce on top of them and then three slices of triangle-shaped Provolone cheese. He placed the sub on a flat metal tray with a long handle, opened the oven door, which made me think of opening the back of a station wagon, and slid my lunch into the heat. He then took a slice of pizza from the counter and slid that into the oven. He gave us our drinks and we sat down at a rickety plastic table next to the front window.

There was no one else in the store. I guess this was what a recession looked like.

The man picked up a copy of the racing sheet. He propped his elbows on the counter and read. I heard a rumbling in the distance which resembled a locomotive engine. It got louder until the vibrations shook the windows of the store.

Chapter Six

A huge Harley Davidson motorcycle stopped in front of the window and chugged until its rider, a long-haired man about the size of Connecticut, cut the engine. He was not wearing a helmet, his hair was parted in the middle, and he had a beard. He looked like a Jesus who had gone over to the dark side.

My aunt watched him indifferently and sipped her tea. I don't think it occurred to her that he might be dangerous. I felt tingles up and down my back.

He came into the store, so my first wish had not been granted. The door frame was barely big enough for him. If the room had been full, it would have gone silent. But it was silent already.

He had a denim vest over a black leather jacket and I watched him go to the counter. There was a picture of Satan or something on the back of his vest with the words "Hell's Angels" stitched in an arc above the picture and "Lowell, Mass" in an arc underneath it. He had a deep scar across his cheek about six inches long. It was carved into his face and it didn't seem to have been stitched up too well whenever it had been treated.

"Gimme a slice," he said in a chainsaw voice. "And a beer."

"Bud or Miller?"

"Miller."

If he had had any hair left, the counter man's would've stood on end. He got a slice from the pizza dish in front of him and put in the oven. He got a beer from the glass case and handed a bottle to the guy.

The biker turned around and leaned against the counter. He had a look, entirely justified, that he was used to terrifying people. He saw me staring at him and I quickly turned my head to pretend I was looking out the window. I was hoping he would leave Aunt Lindy and me alone.

"Meatball grinder and pizza."

"That's our lunch, Aunt Lindy," I said. "I'll get it." I didn't want her to have to be near the biker.

"I'll help, dearie."

My aunt and I went to the counter and I snuck a glance at the biker. I reached for my grinder. My aunt took her slice of pizza, reached into her purse, and paid the man.

"Would you get me a napkin, dearie?" she said to the biker. There was a metal napkin dispenser next to him.

This is the end, I thought to myself.

He looked at my aunt like he was ready to fight, and then shook his head in as much amusement as the scariest person in the world could show.

"Right there," my aunt said, pointing at the silver-colored dispenser. "Right next to the pepper flake jar."

The biker paused, smiled ever so slightly, and pulled a few napkins out. He gave them to my aunt.

"Thank you so much, dearie." My aunt smiled at him like he was an old friend.

You have no idea who you're talking to, I thought as I watched her.

We took our food to the table. Once we sat down, I thought about telling my aunt who she had just spoken to, but I didn't want to bring any more attention to us.

Apparently my aunt had no problem with attracting attention to us because she turned to the counter and said in a loud voice, "Dearie, could you bring me another paper plate?"

The counter man thought my aunt was talking to him, but she was looking at the biker. The counter man raised his eyebrows.

The biker took a paper plate from the stack on top of the glass cover and then he plodded toward us in his heavy boots. The paper plate was in one hand and a bottle of Miller High Life was in the other.

"Is this what you want, grannie?" he said, his voice heavy with sarcasm and grittier than sandpaper. He placed the plate next to my aunt's pizza.

The sarcasm was lost on my aunt. She never used it and rarely noticed it in others. "Oh, I'm not a grannie. I'm an auntie."

"Oh, my mistake," the biker said in a mock formal voice and bowed. "Is that what you want, auntie?"

"Yes, thank you very much."

The biker's boots scraped the floor as he turned away. The Hell's Angels emblem on his denim vest was as clear as a billboard to me, and, I hoped, to my aunt.

"I'm sorry," she said to his back. "I didn't introduce you. This is my nephew. He's a baseball player at school."

If I could have crawled under the table and disappeared, I would have.

The biker turned around and stared at my aunt. I had to hand it to her, she seemed blissfully unaware of the danger he presented. She was a ball of sunshine and assumed the world was a wonderful place.

"What do you do for a living?" she said.

His mouth dropped open. "Oh, odd jobs."

"I'm retired myself. I think Aiden," she pointed at me. "Would like to play professional baseball. Wouldn't you, Aiden?"

I smiled. It was probably the least enthusiastic smile I had ever made.

"Well, thank you again," my aunt said, practically singing it like she was on Broadway. Had there been a piano in the place, I swear she would've started banging out songs.

"Auntie," the biker said and nodded at the both of us.

"Pizza's up," the man at the counter said in a meek voice.

The biker got his slice and I watched him take it out to his motorcycle. I blessed myself.

"Oh, you're right, dearie, we forgot to say grace," my aunt said when she saw me do it.

I didn't tell her I had blessed myself in thanks for being allowed to live another day.

The biker was sitting on his Harley just outside the window from us. He savored both bites of the pizza. He put the Miller to his mouth, tilted his head back, and drained the bottle. He looked through the window at us, held up the bottle, smiled, and tossed it into a trashcan. A guy who was more local than the signs in the road stopped at the motorcycle and talked with the biker. Just a couple of good citizens having a chat on a Saturday.

Chapter Seven

My aunt and I finished our lunch. We went outside and the biker nodded at us as he talked to the local. We crossed the street to the fabric store parking lot to get the Plymouth.

When we got to the car, a guy who needed a shave and who was wearing an apron with yellow cloth measuring tape around his neck pushed open the door to the fabric store. He strode out to us, screaming. "What d' ya think ya doin' parkin' here?"

You could've heard him in New Hampshire.

My aunt blanched and opened her mouth to speak. With her voice cracking, she said, "We just had some lunch."

"Oh, ya did, lady. That's just great. Ya had some lunch."

He was a few inches taller than me and he towered over my aunt. There were loose, stray threads all over the apron. He was an older guy and not in very good shape, but he still scared us. He was just inches away from my aunt's face and said, 'Ya just can't park here, lady."

I thought he was going to bust a vessel in his temple.

My aunt backed up, clutching her handbag to her chest. She was about to cry.

"I got a business here lady!"

Not a very busy one, I thought, looking around the lot that was empty except for our car.

My aunt backed up another step. She was now leaning against the door to the driver's seat. The guy took a step forward, which was when I moved between him and my aunt.

"Whaddya want, you punk!" He jabbed me in the chest with his finger. "I'm gonna call the cops."

I heard a roar behind us that was louder than the Apollo mission. It drowned out everything. I looked toward the noise and saw the Hell's Angel gripping the handlebars of his Harley and stomping down on the bike pedal.

He tore across the street into the parking lot and came up on us like an airplane hitting the tarmac. The noise was so intense that my aunt covered her ears. He brought the bike to a stop and the front wheel was practically touching the legs of the man from the fabric shop.

He cut the engine. All of a sudden it was quiet, but I wasn't sure if that was because I had gone deaf.

The biker swung his leg over the engine and stood up. "You got a problem with my auntie?"

"No." The tailor inched backwards.

"Because I heard some asshole yelling at her. You look kinda like that asshole."

The tailor put his palms up in a surrender gesture. "I was just going back inside."

The biker grabbed a strap on the tailor's apron. "You owe my auntie an apology."

"Sure. Sure." The tailor glanced at my aunt. "Sorry, lady. I was outta line."

My aunt's eye were rimmed with tears. She got a tissue from her handbag and dabbed at them. Then she removed her glasses, wiped them, and put them back on.

"You still here?" The biker said to the tailor.

"Nope, not me." The tailor returned to the fabric store faster than he had come out. The raven-haired girl opened the door for him and cast a nervous look at us.

The biker pointed at Aunt Lindy and nodded.

"You are so kind," she said. "I don't know how to repay you." She reached into her handbag and took out a coin purse. She opened it, found a one-dollar bill, and tried to give it to the Hell's Angel. "It's all the change I have."

The biker held up his right hand as if he were about to take an oath and said, "I gotcha." He looked over at the fabric store and glowered. The raven-haired woman locked the door and disappeared out of sight. The tailor was nowhere in sight. I figured he was packing for Europe.

My aunt reached out to the biker and took his hand. She shook it with both her hands. "Thank you. Thank you so much."

"I'll make sure you get outta here okay." The biker got on his Harley. "You ain't from around here, are you?

I shook my head. "We took Route Three to get here."

"Thought so. Must be other places to get what you need."

We got into the Plymouth. The passenger door thumped shut. My aunt put the key in the ignition and started the engine. The Hell's Angel waited for us.

"You know, I never even asked his name," my aunt said. She turned the car off and got out. "Excuse me, I don't know your name."

"People call me Blade."

"What's your Christian name?"

"I don't use it." He didn't say it threateningly, just as a statement of fact.

"Thank you, Blade."

"My pleasure, auntie."

My aunt got back in the car and we rolled out of the parking lot, which was still empty and probably would be for the rest of the day.

The motorcycle roared again, like a lion announcing that it was the king of the forest. I looked behind me, and Blade was following us. He pointed to his right, trying to signal to my aunt that the road leading back to the state highway went that way.

She didn't see his signal, so I told her. He peeled off in another direction as my aunt made the turn right.

She missed the stop sign.

Chapter Eight

At baseball practice Friday afternoon, Coach had me take batting practice off Travis, a senior and our number one starting pitcher. He's also our number one jerk. Because I'm a freshman he doesn't treat me like a full teammate. He treats Jack the same way. He ignores us in the locker room, at practice, and on the bench in games. I doubled to right against Mariston last week to give us the lead and him the win, and he never congratulated me, slapped my hand or anything when I got back to the dugout.

"Batter up. C'mon," Travis said, even though he had seen me about to step into the batter's box.

I dug my back foot in, tapped the outside of the plate with my bat, and then cocked the bat behind my ear. Travis wound up, kicked his front leg, and burned a fastball at my head. I heard it whiz by as I hit the dirt.

I got up, brushed myself off, and got into my stance.

"Sorry about that. It slipped." Travis said it with a sneer.

Batting practice is supposed to be about working on your timing and swing, not self-defense. The pitcher's supposed to lay it in there for you to hit.

Travis wound up again and rocketed another pitch at me. I jumped into the other batter's box, barely getting out of the way.

Coach didn't see it because he was off in the outfield with the assistant coach hitting fungos. Jack was out there taking fly balls. He had made varsity, too, but didn't get as much playing time in games as me.

"Sorry, man."

It was probably the most insincere apology I had ever heard.

The catcher, Eddie Thompson, a senior, too, said, "Watch yourself." He flung the ball back to Travis. He was friendly about it, like he didn't want me to get hurt. He treated me about the best of anyone on the team, maybe because he made varsity as a freshman, too.

The next pitch came right over the plate and I got it with the fat part of the bat. It felt and sounded perfect and the ball hit the fence on one hop. When I get a little stronger, a hit like that will clear the fence.

It sounded so good that Coach turned around and watched it. Then he gave me a thumbs-up sign, which made Travis furious. Coach was still watching, so Travis threw me another that I could actually hit. I swear it looked like a beach ball coming into the plate. I connected and drove it to the fence in left field. You could see the burn on Travis's face. You're supposed to let guys hit in batting practice, but Travis was taking it personally.

I could guess what was coming. I was determined not to bail on it and give Travis the satisfaction of intimidating me.

Travis wound up, released the ball, and it came straight at me, splitting the batter's box. Even if I had wanted to, I wouldn't have been able to get out of the way.

The ball hit me on the thigh. Travis throws a heavy ball and the pitch felt like a shot put. I hopped out of the box, trying to shake it off. I didn't say anything and I didn't look at Travis. I was going to pretend it didn't hurt, which was going to take some acting.

Coach saw it and called to me. "You okay, Aiden?"

I waved him off, got back in the box, and took my stance. Travis smirked. We had Coach's attention, so he was probably going to groove the next pitch.

He did, and I turned on it. The ball felt like a rocket off my bat. It cleared the fence on a rising line drive to the deepest part of left center, just below the scoreboard. Even guys shagging flies stopped to watch it.

"I don't think you need anymore BP," Coach shouted from the outfield.

Lately, Coach had taken to complimenting me in front of the team. I figured it was because I was the only freshman and he was trying to boost my confidence.

I jogged to the bench, took off my batting helmet, and slipped my bat into the rack. I got my glove and went to the outfield to shag flies. My thigh was throbbing. Shagging flies is my favorite part of practice, just running down fly balls. I could do it all day.

After practice, Tommy Carroll, our third baseman, caught up with me on the way to the locker room. "Don't take it personally with Travis."

I looked at him like I didn't understand.

"He still hasn't heard from any colleges," Tommy said. "At least the colleges his dad thinks he should attend."

"Can't he still play somewhere?"

"He could play as a walk-on, maybe at a JC or small school."

"What's a walk-on?" I said.

"It means you have to earn a place on the team without a scholarship. Travis thinks he had to work a lot harder than you to make varsity. He resents you."

"I thought we were on the same team."

"I don't think Travis sees it that way."

The locker room as quiet when Tommy and I entered. You could feel the tension. I took a towel from the stack on the chair outside Coach's office and went to the shower. By the time I got to my locker, Travis had left. A couple of guys were talking in low voices, but it still felt tense.

Here it was, we were in second place and competing for our school's first league title ever and, from the mood of the locker room, you'd have thought we were in last. At least it was Friday and we had the entire weekend ahead of us. Friday evening is my favorite time of the week.

Chapter Nine

My whole family was waiting for me in the kitchen when I got back from my Saturday morning run. My dad, mom, aunt and sister were standing around the kitchen table, looking like someone had died. I could feel it the moment I walked into the house, and their faces confirmed my feelings.

"What's wrong?" I said.

On Saturday mornings, my mother was usually out by now, shopping for groceries and Eileen would be practicing the piano. My dad would be doing a fix-it project around the house. My aunt would be reading the newspaper and having tea.

They didn't say anything.

"Something's happened," I said, feeling hysteria push at me. I couldn't imagine what it was, but I was sure it was bad.

My mom came to me and put her arm around my shoulders. She looked at my dad.

"Aiden," he said and then stopped.

Eileen started crying. My aunt held her hand.

"It's about Jack," my dad said. "I don't know how to tell you this."

I thought of the worst possible thing that could happen and ruled it out. My dad had taught me to do that, as a way to keep things in perspective.

I had been wrong to rule out the worst because my dad said, 'Jack was hit by a car this morning."

I stared at my dad and suddenly felt nothing. My dad seemed to fade away from me down to the end of a tunnel. Everyone in the room got smaller. The whole room seemed like an out of focus picture.

I started crying, which is something I never do.

Later, after I had stopped weeping and calmed down, my dad came up to my room and sat on the bed next to me.

He told me that Jack had been riding his bike and a guy who had been drinking all night ran over him. The impact had killed him instantly, or so the doctor said. The doctor also said Jack probably felt nothing and didn't suffer.

I wondered, though.

The guy had run the red light in the center intersection of our town and slammed into Jack at fifty miles an hour. At least that's what the police estimated. The driver survived, which made no sense to me.

There was a funeral Mass at St. Camilla's. The casket was closed. I vaguely remember the church was full. Teachers, coaches, teammates, students, and people from all over town were there. Jack's parents let me sit with them and his two sisters. My parents, aunt and Eileen were in the pew behind us. It was an honor for me to sit with Jack's family, but one of those honors I didn't really want because I would rather have had Jack still alive.

I cried for three days after Jack's funeral. My parents let me stay home from school and my mother had taken time off from work. They had offered to let me stay home longer, but I went back to school and walked through the hallways like a robot. I remember going to baseball practice, but not much else, and my batting and fielding must have been on muscle memory since I wasn't thinking much.

Chapter Ten

A few weeks after the funeral, I rode my bike to the town line, where the cemetery was. I hadn't been to the cemetery since Jack had died.

A car sped past me, going in the same direction as me, and I heard someone call out my name from it. The voice was friendly, but it was drowned in the noise of the automobile. I pedaled up the hill and coasted down toward the stone wall that bordered the cemetery.

I came to the entrance and stood up on my bike, pushing hard to go up the incline into the cemetery. The road was choppy and full of potholes and probably hadn't been resurfaced in a decade. It was just wide enough to allow a car to drive up to the grave sites.

Jack's grave was in the newer section, beyond the faded headstones and markers. The town had cleared space for it during the past few years. Jack and I had always talked about graduating together and maybe even going to the same college. It just didn't work out that way.

I got off my bike and walked to the newer section. My throat was tight. I hadn't cried at all since he first died and I didn't think that I would cry now. The three days I cried after he died, I thought I might never stop, but I must have dried up all the tears inside me. It was almost a relief to be choked up now instead of mad or to feel nothing.

Jack's marker was simple, which was something his family wanted. It was just a small square marker in white sandstone. His mother must have visited it recently because there were fourteen red roses lying across the grave. He would have been fourteen this year.

I picked up a rose and smelled it. It was still fragrant. The stem bent in my hand.

"I miss you, Jack," I said aloud to him.

I only stayed a moment or two because it was too weird to be there alone. I had been with my parents when he was buried and I remember my mother put her arm around me and made it kind of better.

A few of the graves had small American flags for the veterans. I saw a car about two hundred feet off to my right. An elderly woman was brushing leaves and grass off a marker in the ground. We were the only people here, the only living people anyway, and it felt like the loneliest place in the world.

For some reason I watched the woman for a few minutes. She didn't notice me looking at her. I guessed it was her husband's grave and I wondered how long they had been married. It must have been a good marriage because she was taking such care of the grave.

I walked my bike all the way to the cemetery entrance and thought about sitting on the stone wall, but I had been here long enough. I mounted my bike and cycled back home. A car beeped at me, but I wasn't doing anything wrong. I was just riding my bike the way you're supposed to in traffic. I saw my father's car in the driveway when I got home. I had been gone longer than I thought.

"Dad's here?" I said to my aunt, who was having tea at the kitchen table.

"Yes, dearie. He's upstairs. You were gone a long time."

I found my dad in his study.

"Dad, I have a question about religion."

He closed the book he had been reading. "Go ahead."

"This kid at school wears a cross and he uses drugs. It seems hypocritical to me."

"I don't hear a question there."

"Why would he do that?"

"I think you're asking why someone who believes in God still has problems."

That wasn't exactly what I was asking, but it was close. "I don't understand why he acts that way."

"Do you think he's allowed to have problems?"

"Yeah." I wasn't sure what my father was trying to say.

"What's really the matter, Aiden?"

"I went to the cemetery today."

My dad got up and put his arms around me.

"Why did God let Jack die?" I didn't say it mournfully or like I was feeling sorry for myself. I just wanted someone to tell me the answer.

I could feel my dad gently shaking his head back and forth as he held me. "I don't know."

I wasn't crying. I didn't feel like crying at all. I just wanted answers that made sense. "I don't understand."

"I don't know if I do, either. Life has hard moments."

"Why does it have to be this way?"

"You're going to need more life experience before you understand," my dad said. "Even then, you may not."

"What if I don't want to wait?"

"You may have to."

"That stinks."

"Sometimes that's how it is," my dad said. He waited for me to say something. "I don't think I answered your question."

"I guess not," I said. "But it's okay."

Chapter Eleven

I had started hanging out with Ryan after Jack died. We had kind of known each other growing up, but we had never been that close. I wasn't even sure how we started hanging out now. We weren't tight, not anywhere near as Jack and I had been, but you need friends, and Ryan fit the bill, I guess.

We were in McDonald's after practice. Ryan didn't play baseball, or any sports, but I had caught up to him when I was walking home. He had asked if I wanted to go to McD's and I said yes, of course, because who doesn't like McDonald's? Besides, dinner wasn't for a little while.

He had asked for a special order without onions, just to make sure the hamburger was hot when he got it, which is pretty smart. For all you know, the burgers could have been sitting there since last week. Not that that would make much difference to me.

We waited to the side for Ryan's order. A working guy in a Red Sox baseball cap ordered a Big Mac and fries from the teenager at the cash register. She must have been from one of the neighboring towns, because I didn't recognize her.

A kid with a ton of acne and who couldn't have been much older than sixteen was working the grill. Working at McDonald's probably wasn't helping his skin, but you work where you can, and it's not like teenagers have their pick of jobs. His paper cap was tilted to one side.

The manager was a tired, middle-aged guy who was wiping down tables in the lobby. Late afternoons at McDonald's in our town are hardly action zones.

A beeping car horn startled me. A Mercury Cougar had parked outside the front doors and some dope was banging on the horn. I looked to the entrance and saw him.

Bernie Kimball came in with two of his freak friends, looking like they'd missed the turn for Woodstock.

I stated at him. Bernie froze. The two kids with him looked nervously at me.

"Let's come back later," one them said to Bernie.

"That's a good idea," I said loudly. "Why don't you come back later?" I took a step closer to Bernie.

I wished the school had let Bernie go on to twelfth grade so he'd be gone this June and I wouldn't have to see him every day this year and next and think about how he got to live and Jack hadn't. But he had lived and not Jack and that was not going to change.

I started churning inside me and tried to tell myself not to lose it. The principal, Mr. Driscoll, had pulled me out of class a short while ago after I had a confrontation with Bernie in the cafeteria. Mr. Driscoll knew me from junior high, where he'd been assistant principal.

Ryan was completely confused. He had never seen me act this way. I'm the last person kids and teachers at school would expect to cause trouble. I wasn't even sure why I was doing it now.

"What's wrong with you?" Ryan said under his breath. He looked around the restaurant.

I ignored him. "Get out," I said to Bernie. "They don't need your business."

That's when the manager stopped wiping tables. He came right up to Bernie and said, "We sure do need you business and we value it, too."

39

Then the manager glared at me. He said to the girl at the register, "This is compliments of the store. Write a receipt for my records." The manager personally led Bernie and his friends to the counter and took their order.

The cashier rang up the order, printed out a receipt, and gave it to the manager. He put the receipt in his pocket and turned to me and Ryan. "When you get your meal, I want you to take it outside. I do not want you in this restaurant."

"I'll eat here if I want," I said.

"Come on, Aiden," Ryan said. "Let's do what he says."

As Ryan said it, two cops came into the lobby. They knew the manager and he said stiffly, "Coffee?"

The cops noticed his manner. One of them said, "What's the matter, Bill?

"I'm having trouble with a customer," he said and pointed at me.

Coach came in at that moment. Talk about rotten luck. He must have stayed late in the locker room after practice and wanted some dinner. He observed the scene, the police, Bernie, the manager who was about to have a stroke, and then me.

"Aiden? What's this about?"

I felt almost as bad about Coach seeing me like this as if my own father had been present.

The manager explained what had happened while I stood there and stewed. He said he was about to have the police remove me from the store.

Coach shook his head. He looked at me and said, "I suggest you cooperate."

The police took me home in their cruiser. They offered Ryan a ride, too, but he said he'd rather walk home. I said I'd rather walk as well, but they said that wasn't one of my options.

It's pretty hard for a police car to be inconspicuous when it parks in front of your house. My whole family was waiting at the front door when I finally got out of the car.

The worst thing was the expression on my dad's face. He was so disappointed in me. I would almost rather have him mad at me.

Chapter Twelve

Coach suspended me from the team. My dad gave Coach his full support. My dad's not the type to make excuses for bad behavior and wouldn't try to cover up for boneheaded stuff. That was the first thing. Then Coach sent me to the guidance office. I assumed my dad was on board with that, too.

The guidance office is part of the administration suite. I went in and waited for Mrs. Martin, my counselor.

Mrs. Martin has been at the high school forever and is around the same age as my parents. Her hair is completely gray and she wears it long, down past her shoulders, like a hippie. The hair made her look older because her skin has no lines and her eyes glow with energy. She was wearing a caftan over a long peasant skirt.

I closed the door behind me after we entered her office. She motioned to two chairs, comfortable, cushioned ones, next to an end table with a softly lit lamp.

"Mr. Driscoll asked me to speak with you," she said. Her voice was soft and gentle. "You're not in trouble. I just thought we could talk."

I had never been in Mrs. Martin's office before. Eileen had, but that was to talk about colleges. Eileen had told me that she was very smart. I scanned the room and saw a diploma from the University of Massachusetts in a black frame behind her desk. There was another one from Lesley College. A couple of small framed photos faced her on her desk. I assumed they were pictures of her family.

"I want to help," she said. "But I need your help, too."

"Is this a therapy session?" My voice was hard and resentful. The comment and the feelings just bubbled up and surprised me.

"No. We're just talking."

I sighed and shook my head at the same time.

"What are you thinking?" she said.

"Nothing."

"You're a good kid, Aiden. We, I, want you to stay on track."

"But," I said. I knew a "but" was coming.

"But, your behavior around Bernie Kimball is unacceptable."

"What happened has nothing to do with school," I said.

"What did happen?"

"I thought you said this wasn't a therapy session." I was getting angry. Or maybe I never stopped being angry and was just getting angrier.

"You sound very angry," she said.

I hate it when people do that. They try to interpret how you're feeling when they can't get inside you and really know.

"You're very angry at me," she said.

I think I hate it more when people try to tell you how you're feeling about them.

"No, I'm not," I said. I was beginning to think that Eileen had been wrong about how smart Mrs. Martin was. "I thought all you did was check report cards and tell kids about college."

I said it rudely. I wanted her to be as upset as I was, yet she remained calm.

The bell rang for the change of classes. I heard the shuffling of feet and murmur of voices through the wall. "I need to go to class."

"I'll write you a pass."

Mrs. Martin seemed to have an answer for everything.

"Do you like baseball?"

What kind of question was that?, I thought to myself. Of course I like baseball. "Why do you ask?"

"Because you're jeopardizing your participation on the team. And for what?" Mrs. Martin paused.

If she was expecting me to have big, personal conversation with her, she was mistaken. But I knew she was sort of right. It was hard to get playing time as a freshman and I was making it even harder by getting suspended.

"Your coach wants to help you. He cares about you as a person as much, more, really, than as a player. He's doing you a favor by suspending you."

Mrs. Martin probably knew nothing about baseball and now she was telling me how coach was doing me a favor.

"I can tell by your expression that you think I'm full of it," she said.

"I didn't say that."

"You didn't have to. It's obvious from the way you're looking at me."

I really wanted to go. If I talked, I figured she might let me leave earlier. "How much baseball have you played?"

"None."

"So?"

"Coaching is about more than teaching you how to play a sport. Your coach is trying to help you cope with life better."

Now Coach was a therapist, in Mrs. Martin's mind. But she had a point. "So what do I have to do?" I said.

"You don't have to do anything."

I hate it when people lead you in a conversation and then won't give you advice that you know deep down they want to give you more than anything in the world. "What do you suggest?" I figured I'd make it easier for her to give me her opinion.

"I think your coach would like to see you resolve your differences with Bernie. Bernie's not really the issue, anyway."

What was that supposed to mean? I thought.

I must have looked as confused as I was because Mrs. Martin said, "Bernie has become a replacement for your anger about a lot of things."

"I don't understand." I really didn't understand and it was probably the first unguarded response I had given her.

"It's more involved than we can cover here, but I would like to recommend someone to meet with you and your family. If you accept, then I think your coach will lift the suspension."

That was the catch. But it was a catch I cared about. Maybe Mrs. Martin was as smart as Eileen said.

Chapter Thirteen

She was a social worker, she said, when I answered the door. She introduced herself as Ms. Friedkin.

She was young, but she hadn't been born ten minutes ago. She was well-dressed and articulate and she sounded like she had done a lot of meetings with a lot of parents and families. The way she dressed she could have been someone who worked in an office like my dad because she had a business suit, nothing like the kind of clothes Mrs. Martin had. I assumed everyone who did her type of work was a free spirit and tried to look the part.

My parents were expecting her and were in the living room, waiting. My mother had set up a tray on the coffee table with cookies and cups for the coffee pot she had placed in the middle of everything.

Her visit, she told my parents, was being paid for by the Massachusetts Department of Corrections. Since it involved an adjudicated youth on her caseload, Bernie, she was permitted to meet with us. With a catch.

There's always a catch, I thought.

I had to agree to meet with Bernie in her presence.

"Does that mean Bernie is coming over here?" I said.

"No," she said. "You'll meet somewhere neutral. Perhaps the school."

My parents talked with her for a few minutes about what had happened with Bernie at McDonald's, like my mother and father didn't already know. Then she asked about Jack and tried me to get to talk about my feelings.

She didn't get very far, but she tried.

We, meaning me, agreed to meet with Bernie at the football field on Sunday afternoon.

The next day, I had time to kill after school since I wasn't playing baseball. I took my street hockey stick and a ball to the school and was slapping shots against one of the brick walls without windows. A kid I had known since elementary school came up to me.

"Hey, Aiden."

I was surprised he spoke to me because we had never been friendly in school. He was just another kid in class, but it's a small high school and a small town.

His name was Robert, but he had taken to referring to himself as "D" for disciple. He was a little weird, not the type of kid I would choose to hang around with. I don't think he liked sports and he was never much good at them in school.

"Are you cool?"

I wasn't sure what he meant. "Yeah, I guess so."

He could tell I didn't understand his real meaning. He smirked. "No, man. What I mean is, do you smoke?"

I couldn't find the words to answer him. He was wearing a denim jacket with a cross on the back with "Jesus Saves" stenciled on the the cross. One of the Jesus freaks at school. I had never been offered marijuana before. I had smelled it before and seen some kids smoking it after school a few times, but nobody had ever approached me about trying it.

I finally said, "I don't smoke."

"C'mon, it mellows you out."

I thought I was mellow enough.

"What are you afraid of?" He said it like I was some kind of weirdo.

"I don't want to smoke anything. Pot. Cigarettes. Nothing."

"What's your hang up?" He almost jeered.

"I play sports."

"So what? Jocks need to get high, too." He took a joint out of his jacket pocket and rubbed it between his fingers.

He must have been desperate for company to be pushing this hard on me. He seemed like a different person than the kid who had been wearing Peanuts t-shirts just a couple of years ago. He had progressively become more open and vocal about his faith, his hair had gotten longer, and he had started hanging out with kids in Bernie's crowd.

I understood now why my dad talked about being involved with positive things after school.

Chapter Fourteen

Coach reinstated me once the social worker let him know she had met with me and my family. It felt great to be back on the baseball field. It seemed like Coach knew how things were going to work out all along

We had a game the day I was back and Coach put me in as a defensive replacement in the late innings.

A senior from the visiting team who was being scouted by the Red Sox and a few other MLB teams came up to bat. He was over six feet tall and built stronger than the Hoover Dam. He was leading the league in hitting and RBIs and last year was an honorable mention for all-state.

Travis was pitching and he was struggling. He had loaded the bases on three walks and had gone to a full count. Travis had to come in with a strike and the batter knew it. He was ready for it and roped a sinking line drive to center.

I ran in on it, reaching down to catch it on a shoestring. It dropped in front of me and skipped over my glove. The left fielder was backing me up and chased the ball to the warning track. By the time he relayed it to the shortstop, three runs were in and we had lost the lead.

I should have played it more conservatively and laid back on the ball. If I had done that, only one run would've scored.

Travis had been backing up home. He walked slowly to the mound and then stood there with his hands on his hips, glaring at me in centerfield.

I felt awful. You make an error like that and it not only hurts the team, but you can't hide.

The next hitter popped up in foul territory on the third base side and we were out of the inning.

I jogged back to the dugout with my head down. Some defensive replacement, I thought. Tommy had made the catch at third and tapped me on the back with his glove when I got to the dugout. "You'll get the next one," he said.

I sat down at the end of the bench.

"Forget about it, Aiden," Coach said. "We need your head in the game."

Travis was sitting a few players away from me. "We're down two thanks to him." He jerked his thumb at me.

"C'mon, Travis," Gary said. "We'll get 'em back."

"He should be on JV." Travis glared at me.

I felt even worse and noticed my teammates were starting to squirm.

"Everyone makes errors," Tommy said to me. "The seniors seem to forget that."

"It's too bad he wasn't the one killed," Travis said, loud enough for everyone to hear.

The dugout went silent. Coach had moved to the on-deck circle and was talking to the leadoff hitter when Travis said it, so he hadn't heard. I gazed out at the field and everything went out of focus.

"Aiden! Aiden!"

I hadn't heard Coach calling me. He had come back into the dugout and I hadn't even noticed. "You're in the hole." He looked at my funny and could tell something was wrong. "What happened?"

I didn't say anything. I just got my bat from the rack and put on my helmet. You could hear the conversations of the students and families watching the game from their seats on the incline around the field because it was so quiet in the dugout. Even Travis had stopped talking.

I hit a homer during my at-bat, the first one of the season for me. It got us within one run, but we ended up losing the game.

I sat by myself in the dugout afterward. Usually Coach makes us all leave together as a symbol of teamwork. For some reason he didn't do it today. I thought about Little League, when Sean taught me how to blouse my baseball pants. I wished I was back there, getting guidance from him. I had always assumed Sean would get a baseball scholarship to college, until Vietnam.

I don't know how long I sat there, but Tommy came back from the locker room to get me.

He took my bat from the rack, got my helmet and glove, and handed them to me. "Come on. Let's go."

We walked back to the locker room. Travis had already showered and changed. He was standing at the edge of the parking lot, waiting for his father, who comes to every game and considers himself Travis's real coach.

Travis's father had been talking to Coach outside the locker room. He finished and walked toward Travis. When he was about ten or twenty yards away, he said, "You should never have walked those hitters." He said so that you could hear it at the tennis courts on the other side of the field.

Travis put his head down.

"You can't get scholarships that way."

"That's what I mean," Tommy said under his breath to me.

"What?" I said.

"Travis's dad expects him to get a baseball scholarship. Except Travis doesn't do much in class. He'd have to be really good to make up for his grades."

I was trying to understand.

"If he had really good grades, with his talent," Tommy said. "He could play at a good small college like Amherst or Williams or something. But his dad doesn't want that."

"What does Travis want?"

Tommy looked at me like I was a freshman. "I don't think that matters."

We heard Travis's father speak again. "How hard is it to throw strikes? Seriously. How hard is it?"

You'd have thought Travis had just lost everything in the world by the look on his face.

"Dad," Travis said as if he had had this conversation a million times with his father. "I'll meet you at the car."

"It'll be some time," his father said. "I need to talk to your coach."

"You," Tommy said to me. "Have a better chance of getting a scholarship and Travis knows it."

We walked down the ramp to the locker room. I felt kind of sorry for Travis, even though he's a jerk. His father came into the locker room behind us and knocked on Coach's door.

I could hear Travis's father arguing with Coach about how Coach was handling Travis. He said he might pull Travis from the team if Coach didn't change what he was doing with him.

Chapter Fifteen

Aunt Lindy and I went back to the fabric store on Saturday. My aunt said she'd wait until after wrestling was finished on television, but I ended up turning if off before it was over.

Watching it had become more and more an empty vigil for Sean's return, sort of like the people who go to Mass and don't pay attention. They're sitting in the pew reading the bulletin during the sermon, and their mind is anywhere but in church. I figured out that I kept following wrestling so I could feel the same way again or magically make Sean reappear, sort of like Professor Tanaka making his opponents mysteriously regain consciousness after he has applied his dreaded sleeper hold. It wasn't working, so turning the television off seemed the best thing to do. Not even Bruno could help now.

Last year my dad even took me to the Garden to see the matches live one Saturday night, the way Sean used to do. He was polite about it, but I could tell from watching him that he felt like he was seeing the end of civilization. Wrestling crowds aren't all that sophisticated. Most of them haven't been to law school or read James Joyce at night. I appreciated him making the effort. I guess that's just what dads do.

During one of the commercial breaks, they announced the card for the next matches at the Garden. Bruno was going to be the main event, but I wasn't interested in going. Not even with my friends. I wasn't going to ask my dad to take me and put him through that again.

My aunt and I drove back to the fabric store and my knuckles weren't too white by the time we got there.

The city hadn't made any capital improvements in the time we had been away.

My aunt parked our Plymouth in front of the store. The tailor remembered the car and my aunt, of course, and greeted us in the parking lot like the Queen had just arrived. He practically laid out a carpet for her.

We went in the store, got what my aunt needed, and came back to the car.

A different kind of welcoming committee was waiting for us in the parking lot. They weren't much older than me, dressed in denim and leather, and outnumbered us. About a half dozen of them had surrounded the car.

"Hey lady, we need some money," a young tough said. He was lean and mean-tempered. He looked to be a few years older than the others.

My aunt reached into her handbag to make a peace offering.

He grabbed the bag out of her hands. "Thanks, lady."

I started to move toward him when two guys grabbed my arms from behind.

"Don't do nuthin' stupid," I heard a voice say behind me.

My aunt was terrified. I was, too.

The fabric store owner saw what was happening, flipped the "Open" sign in the window to the "Closed" side, and pulled down a shade over the front window.

"Let us go," I said. I thought I might pee in my pants.

"Maybe we will. Maybe we won't." The lean one was clearly the leader of the gang. He smiled at the others. They grinned back. "I know you ain't gonna say nuthin' to nobody." He looked at me, pulled up his shirt, and showed me a knife tucked in his pants. "If you want the old lady to keep looking that way."

I started praying silently that they would not hurt Aunt Lindy.

I heard a rumbling in the distance, like the approach of thunder. It gradually got louder until I saw a pack of motorcycles roar past the parking lot. The lean one glanced over at the motorcycles and then looked back at us.

He rifled through my aunt's handbag, found her purse, and took what money was in it. "Not even worth it. Seven bucks." His face turned red. "Give me the keys."

"How will we get home?" Her voice cracked.

"Ain't my problem, you old bag." He snatched the keys from her. He tossed her handbag to the ground. "Let's go," he said to the others. Four of them got into our Plymouth.

I heard the rumbling again and it got loud quickly. A pack of Harleys plowed into the parking lot and formed a wall. Blade was one of the riders and they were all wearing colors. Blade dismounted and walked toward us.

"It's funny," he said to my aunt and me and to the gang, specifically looking at the lean one, as if he could tell right way who was the leader. "I was thinking, this is my auntie's favorite store and that looks like my auntie's car."

He looked at the four hoods in the car. "And I'm wondering what you assholes are doing in her car."

One of them opened the rear door to leave, but before he could get out, one of the other Hell's Angels got off his bike, shoved the guy back in our car, and slammed the door shut. He crossed his arms and stared. "Don't move," he said.

They didn't.

Blade stepped so close to the lean one that he was nose-to-nose with him. "That's a nice handbag on the ground. It looks like my auntie's."

He pulled up the lean one's shirt and grabbed the knife. It seemed he knew the guy, or at least the type. "What's your name?"

"Harold," the lean one said, full of bravado. "But they call me the boss."

"Well, Harold."

Blade punched him in the stomach so hard that I thought his fist might rip through Harold's back.

Harold folded over. His head dropped between his knees and then he collapsed to the pavement. I thought he had stopped breathing.

"What happened here?" Blade said.

"Nuthin'," one of the hoods said.

"Shut up."

The hood did.

By now, all the Angels had left their bikes and were standing just a few feet behind Blade, except for the one next to the car who could have doubled as a less refined Gorilla Monsoon. He appeared to be waiting for an opportunity to pound someone through the asphalt.

There was one other jerk with Harold who was standing next to our car. He tried made a break for it. The Gorilla Monsoon double grabbed his denim jacket, lifted the guy above his head like a human barbell, and heaved him over the top of the Plymouth onto the pavement on the other side of the car. The kid bounced off the asphalt and then lay there. I figured he had busted a couple of bones, at least.

We could all hear him moan.

"Shut up," Monsoon's double said.

"What happened here, Auntie?" Blade said to my aunt.

My aunt told him about the robbery and the threats.

Harold was on his knees and bent forward like he was praying. I wasn't sure if he'd ever be able to stand up again under his own power. At least he hadn't barfed.

Blade looked at the gang. He was still holding the knife. "If you ever go near my auntie again," he said in a whisper and pointed the knife at the car. "I will cut your balls off."

Every guy, including the Angels, instinctively squeezed their legs together.

"Get him outta here," Blade said and poked his boot at Harold. "And get outta the car."

He said it as if the hoods were still in our Plymouth for grins, not because one of the other Hell's Angels had told them not to move.

They got out of our car and picked up the guy who was lying next to it. He was moaning softly. Two of them shouldered him up and dragged him away from the car. A couple of others approached Harold. They hesitated a few feet from him.

"Well?" Blade said.

They picked him up as best they could, but he was still bent over. I thought he actually could not stand up straight.

"How much did they take?" Blade said.

"Seven dollars," my aunt said.

"Find money now," Blade said to the hoods. "If you want to keep your balls."

The hoods quickly emptied their pockets. They each came forward and gave Blade whatever money they had.

"Wait," Blade said and counted the money in front of them. "Fifty-two dollars. I'll consider this part of the civil settlement." He handed the money to my aunt.

"No, no. I just want my seven dollars."

Blade counted out seven dollars and gave it to her. He looked at the hoods. He tucked the remaining forty-five dollars in his denim vest pocket. "This has been a profitable meeting."

The hoods stood there, too afraid to move. Blade squatted on his haunches and then pressed the knife on the pavement until the blade snapped off. He tossed the blade-less knife back at Harold. "You still here?" he said.

The hoods limped away, leaving my aunt and me in the parking lot with six Harleys and Hell's Angels. Blade looked at my aunt. "You gotta find your knitting stuff closer to home."

My aunt smiled faintly. "I don't know how to thank you."

"You saved our lives," I said.

Blade shrugged. "I like to do my part for juvenile delinquency. We'll escort you out."

My aunt and I got in the Plymouth and drove out of the lot with an escort of Harley Davidsons. The Angels followed us to the turnoff for the state highway and then peeled away as we got on the exit ramp.

"You seem so calm, Aunt Lindy," I said as we drove home.

"As worried as I was, I've always felt like I had a guardian angel. I assumed he would protect us."

It was hard to argue with her faith. Angels came in odd forms.

Chapter Sixteen

Ryan invited me to a party that night. The party was at the town line and a little too close to the neighborhood where it wasn't unusual to find a car on blocks in the front yard. There was supposed to be a live band. I was hoping they were good and not just a few guys who never practiced.

We thumbed there. We stood on the side of the road, waiting for someone to stop and drive us the three miles to the town line. A Chevy pickup truck tore past us and I felt a blast of warm, late spring air on my skin. A foreign make motorcycle zipped by us, sounding like a Maxwell House coffee can full of angry bees.

The sky was turning deep gray with evening's onset. I had to be home by ten o'clock, the curfew time my parents had set for me. A muscle car slowed down and pulled to the road's shoulder. It was a yellow Dodge Challenger and I recognized it. It was Warren Cassidy's car. He's one of the seniors and his sister is in my class.

"Hop in," he said. He was wearing a leather jacket, despite the warm night. I had never seen him when he wasn't wearing it. Maybe he wore it to bed. "What are you doing out here, Aiden?"

I didn't know that he knew my name.

"Going to a party," Ryan said.

"I heard about that. The Mullen Brothers' band is playing." He waited for a car to pass and gunned the engine. The car shrieked onto the road.

"Are they any good?" Ryan said.

"Who?"

"The Mullen brothers."

"No, they're terrible. They think calling themselves the Mullen Brothers makes them sound like the Allman

Brothers." He pushed the lighter in dashboard and took a pack of Winstons from his jacket. "But they're cheap. Probably payin' 'em in beer."

The cigarette lighter popped out and Warren took and lit his cigarette. He took the right turn where the road forked. I could see the tree that Bernie Kimball had hit. It was still standing, but the bark was scarred.

We drove on just a little slower than a missile. He came to wide shoulder near the town line and fishtailed to a stop. I think he did it for show. It was just slightly less scary than driving with Aunt Lindy.

The tires crunched the gravel and came to a stop.

"I'll let you out here." Warren leaned across me and pushed the passenger's door open. "It's a little temperamental."

I was surprised to hear him say temperamental.

In neutral, the engine sounded like a huge, beating heart. We got out and he peeled away, spitting gravel back at us. I could hear the vibrating strains of electric guitars once the car was out of sight.

We followed the music to a ranch house along a street of ranch houses that looked the same builder had built the same houses at the same time. The house with the party had a black Mustang in the driveway on blocks. The tires had been removed, and so had the hood. I needed no further evidence that we had crossed the town line.

A massive Harley Davidson was parked next to the Mustang. The front wheel was kicked out on long bars so that the seat leaned back at a forty-five degree angle.

We both hesitated at the driveway's edge.

"This doesn't look like a lot of freshmen are here," I said.

Ryan didn't seem very confident. "This is the address." He glanced at a folded piece of paper in his hand.

"How many kids at school ride Harleys?"

Ryan tried to give me an encouraging smile. He failed. "This is the address."

"Who told you about it?"

"Someone at school."

Someone at school, I thought to myself. That could be any fool. "I don't think this is such a good idea." I started to walk back down the street.

"Wait," Ryan said. "Let's just go in for a few minutes. See if it's any good."

From the sounds of the music, Warren Cassidy's review of the Mullen brothers had been correct.

"I'll give it five minutes," I said.

"Let's go."

I followed Ryan into the backyard of the house. A silver keg of beer was propped on a stack of cinder blocks. I guess they had some blocks left over after putting the Mustang up. The keg was on a patio that looked like the owner had installed it.

A long-haired guy who was as wide as he was tall was standing an arm's length from the keg and was holding a red jumbo-sized plastic cup. Like Warren Cassidy, he wore a leather jacket despite the heat, except he had a denim vest over it with a Hell's Angel logo.

I walked to the perimeter of the yard, along the chain link fence that separated it from the neighbors. Ryan stuck with me. I think he was as worried as me, but he wasn't showing it.

Playing street hockey under the lights at the town tennis courts was looking a lot more attractive.

"Give it a few minutes," Ryan said.

We went to the very back of the yard and sat at the base of the fence in some tall grass that hadn't been trimmed since whenever the lawn had last been mowed. I scanned the crowd. There were maybe forty or fifty people and none of them were our age. I wondered who had told Ryan about the party. Maybe someone with an older brother or sister. It didn't look like adult parties were much fun, and it was our lousy luck that a member of Hell's Angels was here.

Everyone was smoking, cigarettes and pot. We were not with the cross country crowd.

The band was playing something that was a muddle of notes. It was sloppy and the amplifiers were distorted. Not Jimi Hendrix I'm-experimenting-with-sound-distortion, but we're-lousy-and-can't-afford-better-equipment distortion.

They might have been up there rehearsing from the way they played, just trying out new songs that no one in the band knew or had practiced. I would make them pay for their beer.

These weren't high school kids, either. They were adults, with day jobs I assumed, but they were long-haired, gaunt, and grungy and probably did not work at a law firm. They started and stopped a song a few times and I thought I recognized the opening chords. In the middle of the first verse of the song, which I still couldn't name, the lead singer, who was wearing a purple bandana around his head, stopped and said into the microphone, "We're gonna take a break."

A few people clapped, probably girlfriends, or someone as thankful as me that they had stopped.

Ryan had sold me on the party. It was going to be so cool, he had said. It turned out to be boring just sitting here listening to no-talent musicians and watching adults drink beer. I could go to a Patriots game and do that. At least I could see some football.

People kept arriving, though, and they didn't seem bored. They were talking loud and smiling and laughing like it was the best party in the world. During the band's break, the backyard filled up with one hundred or more people, including another biker.

It was Blade. He cut through the crowd like Moses parting the Red Sea. Nobody got within a couple of feet of him and you would've thought the party was in his honor. He went to the keg and cut to the front of the line. Nobody complained. He filled a red plastic cup, chugged it down, and then filled it up again.

About fifteen minutes later, the band came back to a smattering of applause. The drummer kicked the bass a couple of times and tapped the cymbals. The two guitarists slung Fenders over their shoulders while the bass player fiddled with the amplifier controls behind him.

"We're the Mullen brothers," the lead singer said. He took the microphone from the stand and whirled the cord around like a lasso.

A woman shrieked. Girlfriend, I assumed.

"We'd like to do an original." The lead singer looked back at the band and shouted a four-count.

Great, I thought, *as if your covers aren't bad enough. Now you're going to inflict an "original" on us.*

The music was a lot louder this go-round. It wasn't any better or any less distorted, but it was louder. The neighbors must have hated it.

Ryan and I hadn't moved from our place at the back of the yard at the base of the fence. I needed to go, but there was no way I was going to ask for the bathroom. I was wondering how everyone else was able to hold it. I felt like we were two kids at recess hanging around the basketball court, waiting for someone to invite us to play. I hadn't seen anyone that I knew, not even an older townie or two. I wondered again how Ryan had a connection to all this. It was eight-thirty and I was thinking about getting home before ten.

If it weren't for the fact that the evening was starting to feel dangerous, for reasons I couldn't quite say, it would have been one of the most boring nights of my life.

It was then that Blade caught sight of me.

Chapter Seventeen

Blade had been anchored to the keg, along with the other Hell's Angel. But he left it and started toward me.

"Jesus," Ryan said. "What did we do?" When Blade got closer, Ryan whispered to me, "Look at that scar on his face."

I stared at Blade. As far as I had seen, he had one facial expression, so it was pretty hard to read his mood.

"Your auntie know you're here?" he said in a voice that sounded like a bucket of rattling nails.

"No, sir."

"This ain't no place for you. Get lost."

I nodded like a bobblehead. Blade turned around and started to walk away.

"We just got here," Ryan said under his breath. "The party's just getting good."

I thought for a moment that Ryan must be living in a parallel universe because I wasn't at the same party he was talking about. I was so ready to leave that I thought this must be what hostages felt like.

"Are you gonna let him scare you off?" Ryan raised his chin at Blade's back.

I looked at Ryan in disbelief. "Of course I am."

At that moment, Blade turned and said, "You still here?"

"Nope," I said, and gripped the top bar of the chain link fence I was leaning against. I swung myself over like Victor Rivera entering the ring.

The backyard abutted a wooded area that was thick with spring growth. I hit the ground on the other side of the fence and felt twigs crack under my feet. I moved quickly through the woods and ran into a low-hanging pine branch that scraped my face. In the dark, it was hard to see beyond the trees right in front of me.

I remembered how much I needed to go. I got behind a thick-trunked tree and peed. I heard a dog barking from one of the neighbor's houses. I hoped their yard was fenced in because it didn't sound like a small dog.

A fog horn blasted at me from the other side of the tree. At least it resembled a fog horn. I was still taking care of business and looked around the tree. A Doberman was standing on its hind legs with its front paws on the top of the chain link fence surrounding its yard. Its bark was louder than the band.

"Stupid dog! Shut up!" I heard someone shout from the house.

That only made the dog madder, which was just what I didn't need.

Just stay in your yard, I thought.

I finished and moved in the direction of the street. I could faintly make out lights a few hundred yards off and figured that was the way out. The wood's floor crackled under each step I took. I looked back at the dog and it leaped over the fence. At me.

He, she, it was no more than thirty or forty feet from me and was closing ground fast.

I thought about how much I hadn't done yet in my life. But only for a second or two. I grabbed another low-hanging branch on a pine and pulled myself up. It was one of those old pine trees that's probably been around since before World War One, so it was tall and had a bunch of branches to climb on. Maybe too many, because it was getting awkward to move higher.

I was willing to deal with awkward over having my leg amputated.

The Doberman lunged at me and caught the back of my sneaker with his teeth. I nearly lost my grip in the terror. The dog dropped back to the ground, barking insanely, and jumped again.

I got up a few more branch levels and was out of his reach now. I hoped. I considered that the dog might be able to climb trees. Or maybe he'd chew through the trunk and knock the tree down.

"You stupid dog!" I heard the same voice shout. "Where are you?"

The Doberman was circling the tree, barking at the huge threat I posed. *Go eat a burglar, you crazy dog*, I thought.

I climbed higher. The branches and growth were thick enough that I was camouflaged from ground view. At least to humans. This dog probably had Superman X-ray vision, though.

I heard heavy footsteps, like someone in boots. "Come here, Patton."

It figured its name was Patton. Panzer must have already been taken.

The dog stopped barking and stood at the base of the tree, guarding it. The owner grabbed the dog's collar. He looked up, and I hoped he wouldn't see me.

"What are you doing? Chasing a squirrel? Come on." He dragged the dog back to the house.

I held onto a branch and felt my chest heaving. My hands were covered with pitch, pine needles had fallen down the back of my shirt, and my face stung. Some party. It would be easier to wrestle at the Garden next time Bruno comes.

I waited to hear a door shut and then climbed down. I stopped about ten feet from the ground, just in case the dog had snuck back without its owner knowing. I waited, like a moron, for another five minutes.

I grabbed onto a lower branch and swung myself to the ground. I ran as soon as I felt the earth. I bounced off trees and got smacked in the face by branches more times than a punch-drunk boxer.

I made it to the street, crossed it, and stuck my thumb out. Had I know what I looked like, I would have just walked the whole way.

Warren Cassidy's Challenger appeared on the road. The headlights shone in my face and I closed my eyes to the glare. He pulled to a stop and pushed open the passenger side door.

"Jesus, what happened to you?"

"I lost a fight with Mother Nature."

"Mother Nature and then some. You're all bloody."

I looked in the side view mirror of the car. I looked like a young Frankenstein. I was lucky Warren had been willing to stop.

"This happen at the party?"

"Sort of."

I got in and he drove me to the town center. I decided to make conversation on the way. "Where are you coming from?"

"My aunt's house," he said. "I was helping her move some furniture. Pretty boring way to spend a Saturday night, huh?"

"I think it's a nice thing to do. Better than a stupid party with the Mullen brothers."

"Didn't I tell ya they were awful?" He pushed the lighter in on the dashboard. "You don't smoke do you?"

"Nope."

"Didn't think so, playing baseball and all. Mind if I do?"

"It's your car and you're giving me a lift."

He turned down the radio, which was playing a hard rock song on a station from Worcester. I liked the song and the station. It was the one I usually listened to. We were the only ones on the road.

"It's a quiet town," Warren said.

"Yeah it is."

"I like it that way."

I nodded. I thought about how I got involved with Ryan in the first place. He wasn't really a close friend. I guess he was just someone to fill the void left when Jack died. But he couldn't replace Jack. No one could, I guess.

Warren dropped me at the end of my street and I thanked him for the lift. I walked to my house from there.

Chapter Eighteen

I could hear the television in the den when I got into the house. I went in and my aunt was in a rocking chair watching a detective show. She loves detective stories. I guess most people do, since every program at night is one.

"Hi dearie. What happened to your face?" There was no alarm or worry in her tone, just a request for information.

"It's a long, stupid story."

My dad came into the den as I said it. He didn't react as calmly as Aunt Lindy. "What happened?"

I saw no reason to make up a story. The truth would be easier to remember anyhow, rather than some lame tale I made up. "I."

Before I could finish, my dad said, "Have you been smoking?"

That really upset me. I think smoking is the stupidest habit in the world and I figured my dad knew me better than that. But I had to give it to him that the circumstantial evidence wasn't leaning my way.

"No, Dad. I was at a party where everyone else was."

"You have a fight?"

"With a tree. And a dog. I think I lost them both."

My mother came in to the den. "Aiden, your face." She reached for my cheek and caressed it with her hand. She didn't seem to care that she'd get blood on her. "Let's go in the kitchen and clean that up."

We all went to the kitchen, even my aunt, and I knew she must have thought it was important to give up seeing the end of her television program.

I sat at the table while my mother went to the bathroom to get some medical things. My aunt took a seat next to me. My dad stood by while my mother laid out some cotton balls, witch hazel and a face cloth on the table.

"This will sting," she said. She dabbed my face with a cotton ball soaked in witch hazel.

She was right. It felt like little flashes of fire.

"Do you want to explain what happened?" my father said.

"I went to that party with Ryan, like I told you. Except it turned out it was a party for adults. There were no freshmen there. I don't know who told Ryan about it."

"Was there drinking?"

"Yeah, a lot." I looked at my dad. "But I didn't drink. You can smell my breath."

"We believe you, dearie," my aunt said.

"I would've smelled it by now," my dad said.

My mother wiped my entire face. The witch hazel made my skin feel tight. Then she took the face cloth to the kitchen sink, ran it under the faucet, wrung it out, and brought it back to the table. She wiped my face with it. It felt really good to be cared for by her.

"Where was this party?" My dad's tone was like the one he has with clients whose stories he's skeptical of.

"Maple Street."

"Maple? How'd you get out there?"

"We thumbed. Karen Cassidy's brother gave us a ride."

"Karen's a nice girl," my mother said and looked at my dad. I think she was trying to keep him calm.

"And you got home by walking?"

"No, Karen's brother picked me up again. A coincidence."

My dad seemed like a tired priest who had heard too many confessions. In his line of work, he probably hears a lot of stories that just make him shake his head. I recall he once said that people have an extraordinary ability to put themselves in dumb situations. "Whose idea was this party?"

"Ryan's."

"I assume Ryan looks as rugged as you."

"He stayed at the party. I left without him. I should've left after five minutes."

My mother gently held my chin between her thumb and index finger and regarded her nursing work. "You look good as new."

"Thanks, Mom."

"Why didn't Ryan leave with you?" my dad said.

I think he was in his lawyer frame of mind now.

"He wanted to stay," I said. "Even when Blade told me to leave."

My aunt perked up. "Blade?"

Blade had become a folk hero of sorts in our family. My mom and dad seemed to listen more closely, too.

"He came to the party a little after we did and saw me. He told me to leave, so I did. I went the back way, through the woods, which is how I got so cut up. I couldn't see in the dark very well and kept running into branches. Then the dog chased me."

"The dog?" my mother said.

"Yeah. A Doberman. I climbed a tree to get away. That's why my hands look like this." I held open my hands, palms up, and showed her the black pitch all over them.

"Let's try this," she said and poured some witch hazel on the face cloth. She wiped my palms. Some of the pitch started to come off.

"I wish I had just stayed home. I wish I could just play street hockey at the tennis courts with Jack again. Ryan doesn't want to do things that I like to do."

My mom, dad, and aunt looked at me. I could see my mother sigh and even my dad seemed affected.

"It's hard to find good friends," I said. "I really miss Jack."

Chapter Nineteen

We were waiting in the depot, my aunt and my sister and me, for the connecting bus into Cambridge. Eileen had been wanting to see Harvard's campus, even though she herself thought it was a reach, at best. Every year, every good student in our town's high school senior class feels obligated to apply to Harvard, just on the off-chance they get in, if only for bragging rights.

The depot sat on an old state route into Boston that was more important before the Mass Pike and Route 128 and the interstates were built. Now, it shared the block with old family businesses that repaired sewing machines, mixed paint, and sold pizza and cigarettes, and it seemed that time had stood still for them.

We had already been to the seven o'clock Mass with the rest of the fanatics who got up early for church. We had decided to take the bus because my aunt wasn't keen on trying to park in Harvard Square and my sister and I weren't keen on watching her try to park in Harvard Square.

My aunt had really wanted to come, for some reason. My parents thought it would be a good idea for her to accompany me and Eileen. Besides, they had already taken Eileen on a million campus tours during the past year.

The buses were on a Sunday schedule, which meant they came every decade or so. We had time to kill until the next one.

I recognized two townies who were about ten years out of high school and nowhere near to having steady jobs, as far as I or anyone else could see. Normally they're in the parking lot of the shopping center in our town, hanging out with the other townies. They spend more time there than the people who work at the shops. Eileen was reading a brochure she'd received from Harvard and my aunt was knitting. I don't think they took note.

The depot was a transfer point for buses going in and out of Boston, so I guess the townies had some reason to be here. The building was shaped in a cinder block and about as attractive. A chain link fence surrounded the bus yard and was neighbor to thorn bushes and scrub plants that hadn't been pruned since the Eisenhower Administration.

I noticed a short, scrawny man with a scraggly growth on his chin, long red hair in a ponytail and baggy cargo shorts. He was wearing a sleeveless t-shirt and was sitting at the counter eating an egg sandwich on toasted white bread. He had coffee in a white ceramic mug and a half-empty bottle of ketchup was next to his plate.

He was the main drug dealer in our town, or so I had heard the freaks at school say about him.

He always carried a faded Army green denim backpack. He was well known in certain circles in eastern Massachusetts, none of them respectable. He lived without trappings or possessions, at least none that anyone ever saw, and got around primarily on a bicycle. He did not appear to have any friends or associates and came and went like a ghost.

The counterman poured some more coffee into the dealer's mug. He was a middle-aged guy with flabby cheeks and lines that had been carved into his face by years of hard work and relentless bills. He had on a white paper hat and a grease-stained apron that might have once been white. He looked like he had been working there since Adam.

I watched the two townies sit down next to the dealer. The dealer didn't look up from his plate.

"What are ya havin'?" the counterman said.

"Coffee."

"Hey big spender," the counterman said, "We got a two dollar minimum."

"Fancy place, huh?" One of the townies pointed at the dealer's plate. "Gimme a sandwich like him."

The counterman looked at the other guy.

"Same."

"Right up." The counterman poured coffee into mugs for them and then turned his back and poured beaten eggs onto the griddle. The eggs sizzled and grease spit up on his bare forearms. He didn't react, as if his skin had no nerve endings.

A few other people were sitting on a bench in the waiting area with us, most of them pensioners. One of them opened up his copy of the *Record* to the baseball scores. A stringy old man in a fedora sitting next to him glanced over the guy's shoulder at the newspaper.

"Think the Sox'll finally win this year?" he said.

"I don't know. They look pretty good, though."

"Yeah, we'll see, I guess. Them Yankees will be hard ta beat."

The dealer left the rest of his sandwich on the plate along with a quarter tip. He got up and went out through the door leading to the street.

The counterman brought the sandwiches.

"Pay up front."

One townie took out a five-dollar bill from his wallet and paid him.

"Big spender," the counterman said as he picked up the quarter next to the dealer's plate. He put the tip in his pocket. He took the plate, fork and coffee cup.

"Anything else for you guys?"

"Nope."

The counterman took the dirty dishes to a sink next to the grill and hosed them off.

"You gonna leave a tip?" I heard one say.

"Nope. Guy did hardly nothin'."

They went out to the bus waiting area.

The counterman turned around from the sink, saw they had left, and got their plates. "No tip? Chiselers." I heard him say.

One of the pensioners had watched them leave. "These young guys don't appreciate work," he said.

"No, they don't," the counterman said and wiped down the counter.

A few minutes later, the two townies burst into the depot waiting area, slamming the door open. My aunt and sister jumped in their seats.

The two guys were frantic and lunged for the front door on the street side. The counterman took a mop, stepped out from behind the counter, and stuck the mop out to trip them. A cop came as they fell to the floor.

Two others entered from the street entrance. The cops handcuffed the townies. I heard one of the cops read them their rights.

"Stiff me on a tip, will ya?" The counterman glared at the two townies, picked his towel from the counter, and wiped his hands.

"They should have tipped him," Eileen said quietly to me.

I guess she had been paying attention.

My aunt, sister and I watched the police arrest the guys and take them away. Then we boarded the bus to Harvard Square, which arrived before I needed to start shaving on a daily basis.

The three of us got off in Cambridge and walked through Harvard Yard among the academic buildings and the residence houses. Aunt Lindy seemed more excited to be there than Eileen. I was making notes in my head for myself, for when I would be old enough to apply to college. Maybe I could play baseball here.

"I'm so glad you have a chance to go here," my aunt said.

"I'm not sure how much of a chance I have," Eileen said with uncharacteristic modesty. "But I'm going to apply."

"Even applying is something. I never considered going to college."

"Why not?" I said.

"It was a different era, dearie. Working girls like me got jobs after high school. Our whole family did, except for your father."

"Why not Dad?" I said. My dad doesn't talk much about himself, so it was interesting to get a different perspective.

"He was the youngest," my aunt said. "And a very good student. I encouraged him to go to college. I even promised him that I would work to help pay for his tuition if he was accepted."

"And he was," Eileen said.

I was pretty sure Eileen knew most of the story already, but I think she was enjoying hearing Aunt Lindy tell it. I also was beginning to realize why my dad would do anything for Aunt Lindy.

"I'm so proud of you," Aunt Lindy said hugged Eileen.

We walked around campus for a while, as much for my aunt as for Eileen, and got a bus back home. I was due at the football field.

Chapter Twenty

Two things I know are true. You can see a lot from the top row of bleachers and there are few places emptier than a high school football field on a spring Sunday afternoon.

The sun was bright and the band of my varsity baseball cap was soaking through. A gaunt man was jogging on the track in a matching gray fleece suit. He moved nearly as slow as if he were walking and it seemed he was punishing himself more than he was getting exercise.

From my vantage point I could see in any direction. I wanted it that way, so that I would be able to see Bernie and his social worker coming. I heard an automobile engine and saw a Chevrolet take a parking slot outside the locker room.

A large, heavy-set black man in a shirt and tie got out of the car. He scanned the area, first looking at baseball diamond and then toward the football field. He walked to the entrance in the chain link fence surrounding the field.

I watched him swing open the gate and carefully close it behind him. He walked about ten yards along the brick-red rubberized track surface and stopped. The jogger struggled past him and nodded at the man as if he hoped he would tell him that he could stop running.

Another car arrived, a small Dodge sedan that had to be at least ten years old. It parked next to the Chevrolet. The driver's side door opened and I could make out that it was Ms. Friedkin, who had come to our house. Then Bernie Kimball got out of the car. I had assumed Bernie would come alone.

The man in the tie waved at them and waited. Ms. Friedkin and Bernie walked to the football field. Bernie's left leg dragged behind him and it occurred to me that simply walking was one of the biggest hassles in his life.

They met the man on the track and the three of them walked along it toward the home team bleachers where I was sitting. As they got closer, the man in the tie no longer looked heavy-set but like an athlete who'd gotten a bit out of shape. He was built strong through the shoulders and had probably been a weightlifter or a football player. A linebacker, I guessed. He was thirty-five or forty years old, but I couldn't exactly tell. Anyone older than college age looked pretty much the same age to me.

Bernie was wearing a black Pink Floyd Dark Side of the Moon t-shirt. The social worker was in a business suit and must have been boiling under the sun.

They stopped at the bottom of the bleachers.

"Aiden," Ms. Friedkin said and shielded her eyes from the sun. She waved for me to come down to them.

I hesitated. Bernie shifted uncomfortably on his feet. The man and the social worker waited patiently, like they had the whole afternoon.

"Come on, brother," the man said. "Meet us halfway."

I stood up and walked down the middle bleacher aisle. When I got to the track level, Ms. Friedkin smiled at me and told me how glad she was to see me. It sounded like she may have meant it.

"This is Mr. Frazier," she said.

"Please to meet you, Aiden," he said and swallowed my hand in his. "I'm Bernie's probation officer."

I said nothing. I wasn't sure what a probation officer did. Bernie regarded me suspiciously. I guess I would've felt the same way if I had been in his shoes.

"What happened?" Mr. Frazier said, looking at the cuts on my face.

"Oh, I had some trouble in the woods and the dark last night," I said.

"Have you seen a doctor?" Ms. Friedkin said.

"My mother took care of it. She's sort of an honorary nurse."

"Okay," Mr. Frazier said, like he didn't want any more information. In his line of work, he probably heard a lot of stories that were true, but were so screwy that he probably wished that they were fiction.

"Could we go to the other side of the field where it's shady," Ms. Friedkin said.

The four of us walked silently across the middle of the football field. I had been on a lot of baseball fields, but the distance from one end zone to the other seemed like miles.

A row of old pine trees shaded a section of the bleachers in the top row, near the press box tower. We went up to the shaded area and sat down. I sat in the row just below them with my back to the field, looking up at them.

Ms. Friedkin must have sensed my doubt. "You can trust Mr. Frazier," she said.

"Trust is earned," Mr. Frazier said.

"I know this is difficult," she said. "But if you both try, things will be better."

I was skeptical.

"Bernie has been on probation since his car accident," Mr. Frazier said. "He has to meet certain conditions. One of those is no drugs or alcohol."

I nodded.

"He has been meeting those conditions," Mr. Frazier said.

I was about to say something smart aleck about not wanting to hear a sales pitch, but the probation officer was the kind of guy you didn't mess around with.

"I think what Mr. Frazier is trying to say is that Bernie is trying hard to make the most of a second chance." Ms. Friedkin smiled a little sadly at Bernie.

"He's not permitted to drive, either," Mr. Frazier said. "He's been meeting that condition, as well."

Bernie nodded along. "I walked to McDonald's that night...."

He didn't finish and I felt ashamed.

"Bernie," Ms. Friedkin said. "Do you want to say what it's like being on probation?"

Bernie didn't look like he wanted to say, but he spoke up anyhow. "It's...it's...."

He seemed so sad and lonely to me.

Mr. Frazier took over. "Can you imagine what it's like to know that your worst mistakes are common knowledge among all your peers?"

I shook my head slowly. I had no idea how it must feel. "Everyone knows about Jack."

"That must be hard," Ms. Friedkin said.

"It bites," Bernie said.

We all looked at him.

"No one will sit with me at lunch. Most days I just go outside until it's over. If I do go to the cafeteria, people move away from me." His eyes teared up and he looked away from us. "It's hard," he said, after an interval.

"What's hard?" Mr. Frazier said.

"To make friends. The only ones who accept me are the freaks."

I had always thought he had chosen to be with the kids who used drugs. It never occurred to me that he believed he had no alternative.

"Some kids get pushed to the margin. Sometimes it's due to their choices," Mr. Frazier said. "Sometimes it's not. It's our job to keep young people like Bernie connected to their community."

"Some kids can go through four years of high school without saying a word in class." Ms. Friedkin looked at me.

"I understand you play varsity baseball," Mr. Frazier said. "That's pretty unusual for a freshman. That's impressive. I also know what happened with your friend."

"I don't want to talk about this."

"You don't have to," Ms. Friedkin said. "But at least hear us out."

"What do you think it's like for Bernie?" Mr. Frazier said.

"I don't know," I said. "Ask him."

"I know everyone thinks I'm a loser," Bernie said.

"That's not true," she said.

"Yes, it is. You know it is. I walk through school and it's like I don't even exist."

Everyone got silent. I felt pretty mixed up inside and I was guessing Bernie and everyone else did, too. I got up because I didn't want to listen anymore. I wanted to say that things were tough all over, but I held myself back. Mr. Frazier held up his hand. I sat back down.

"The cool kids like you can't possibly understand," Bernie said.

I had never thought of myself as cool. I was just another freshman.

"I'm supposed to graduate this year."

I listened, not sure what I as supposed to say.

"I'm not saying what Bernie did wasn't serious," Mr. Frazier said. "And I'm not saying what happened to your friend wasn't painful. But you both are paying and paying and paying for your circumstances."

I wasn't sure what Mr. Frazier meant. He noticed it.

"Bernie has hurt people with his actions, and now he is struggling to make up for it. You've suffered a loss, but punishing Bernie for it isn't going to help."

"I'm not...."

"Consciously, anyway," Mr. Frazier said.

"Could you explain this in a way I can understand?" I said.

"I think Mr. Frazier is trying to say that you are taking out your feelings on Bernie. He has become a replacement for the people who.... He has replaced the other driver in your mind."

I put my head down and traced a random design on the bleacher bench with my finger. I glanced at Bernie. He seemed like this was the last place on earth that he wanted to be. He also seemed so desperate, though he didn't say a word.

"Your coach told me about you, Aiden. Says you're a great kid. Big-hearted, thoughtful, with talent to go far in baseball. And he's noticed a change in you."

"You know Coach?" I said.

"We went to school together. I played football with him at Howard." Mr. Frazier watched my reaction. He could tell that Coach's opinion really mattered to me. "It would help everyone, you included, if you could settle your differences with Bernie. He's not really the issue in your life."

I wanted to say something, but nothing came out. Mr. Frazier, Ms. Friedkin, and Bernie gave me a couple of minutes, but I still said nothing.

"I think we've taken enough of your time," Mr. Frazier said and got up. When he stood up, a row above me, he seemed about ten feet tall. He stepped down a row and put his hand out. I shook it. "Is there someplace in town where I can get something to eat on a Sunday afternoon?"

"There's a pizza place just beyond the town center."

"Thanks for the recommendation." He shook my hand again.

"I'll drop you at your house," Ms. Friedkin said to Bernie. She turned to me. "Would you like a ride?"

"No, thank you. I'll just stay here for a minute."

They started down the steps of the bleachers.

"I used to watch my brother train here," I said aloud.

Mr. Frazier stopped and looked at me. "Are you close to your brother?"

"I used to be."

Mr. Frazier waited like he wanted me to say more.

"I don't know why that just came to mind," I said. "Never mind. I guess I'll see you around.

All three of them stood there, expecting me to say something else. I didn't. They descended the bleachers and I watched them walk on the track to the gate. I sat there until their cars drove away. I thought of Jack and how often we had sat together in these bleachers. The meeting hadn't resolved much of anything, as far as I could see. Maybe Ms. Friedkin and Mr. Frazier felt differently about it. It seemed like a waste of time to me.

I watched their cars disappear behind the trees.

Chapter Twenty-One

At school on Monday, Ryan came to my desk before class had started. "You shouldn't have split."

I doubted him more than if he'd said he was going to give me twenty bucks.

"The pigs busted the party," he said.

It was jarring to hear him say "pigs." I glanced around the room to check if anyone was listening.

"They brought in a canine unit, man." Ryan was visibly excited. "It was so cool."

"I don't want to talk about this now," I said.

"What's your problem? Lighten up."

I was aware that a couple of kids near us were watching and listening but trying to pretend that they weren't. High school kids are so nosy.

"What happened to your face?" he said.

"Long story," I said and tried to ignore him.

The teacher came in just before the bell. We took our seats and the morning announcements came over the public address system. It was Mr. Driscoll's voice. It was pretty cool having him as a high school principal after having him in junior high. I liked him then and he had done nothing to change my mind. He asked us to stand for the Pledge of Allegiance.

Everyone stood except for Christopher Thompson. He was protesting the military's continuing presence in Vietnam even though a peace accord had been signed. I respected him for having the courage to stand out from the crowd like that, especially since I knew that he had thought a lot about it and wasn't just trying to be contrary or to get attention. He doesn't say much otherwise. His parents are Quakers and go to church in another town, which shows commitment. St. Camilla's is only a few hundred yards from the high school and I hear kids complain about having to get there for Mass.

After the announcements, the teacher let us talk for a few minutes. Ryan had a seat near mine and apparently wasn't finished talking about the party.

"It was major," he said. "The pigs busted people and there was almost a brawl. You know that biker with the scar? They arrested him."

"Look," I said. "I don't want to talk about it now." I said it a little too loud because the teacher looked at me.

"Aiden," she said. "Is there a problem?" She noticed the cuts on my face, but didn't say anything.

At practice, Coach asked me why my face was so cut up. I told him the truth and hoped he wouldn't bench me or, worse, cut me.

"Were you drinking?"

"No, sir. I don't do that."

"And don't start," he said. "I've seen alcohol ruin a lot of futures."

"I know."

I wasn't sure if Coach was talking about Jack.

Chapter Twenty-Two

I told my dad just before dinner about Blade getting arrested at the party. The source was Ryan, so I wasn't sure how accurate it was, I had said, but I thought my dad should know. My aunt overheard me and went into my dad's study after I went downstairs.

My dad came downstairs with my aunt. He appeared to be on a mission. "Get your homework and bring it, if you have any. We may be a while."

"Where are we going?" I said.

"Boxwood."

"What's the matter?" my mother said. "We're having dinner in half an hour."

"Can you hold it?" my dad said. "I need to go to the police station. To see Blade." My dad paused. "I wish I knew his real name."

My mom understood after he explained the situation. Blade had helped Aunt Lindy twice now and my dad felt a moral obligation to help him out. After what Aunt Lindy had done for him, I don't think there's much of anything he wouldn't do for her. "I'll keep it warm for you two."

The police station in the neighboring town was a small, one-story brick building on the town common. The sergeant, a middle-aged fat guy, was sitting at a desk.

My dad was still in his suit. He came in like he owned the station.

The sergeant sat up straight. "Can I help you?" He said it as though he didn't encounter too many people in a suit on a typical day, mainly surly types being brought in on charges.

"I'd like to speak with a person I believe you are holding." My dad gave the sergeant his business card. It was a Boston-based law firm with an excellent reputation, not that I thought the sergeant knew that. But I've seen my dad's business card and it's pretty impressive, at least to a freshman.

"Who's that?" The sergeant got defensive, but not rude. My dad didn't appear to be the kind of person you could bully or railroad.

"He goes by the name Blade."

The sergeant stiffened. You could almost see the wheels turning in his head, trying to figure out how my dad could be connected to a member of Hell's Angels.

He got up and took a set of keys from the desk drawer. "Follow me." He led us to the back of the station, unlocked a door, and took us into the holding area. There were four cells. Three of them had occupants, none of whom looked out of place.

Even though he had never met him, my dad recognized Blade. "I'd like a private word, if possible."

"Sure. Sure, sir. I'll be right outside, if you need me." The sergeant left the holding area.

"Blade?"

Blade looked up from his bed where he was sitting. "Who's asking?"

"My name is McManus. I'm an attorney." My dad took out a business card and held it between the bars for Blade. "I looked into your case."

He reached up from the bed, took it and read it. "So?"

"You came to the aid of my sister twice, at a fabric store. I understand you're in some trouble and I may be able to help you. My line of work is right up your alley."

Blade stood up and came to the bars. He recognized me. "Your son?"

My father nodded. I sort of smiled. It's hard to smile when you're outnumbered by criminals, even if they're locked up.

"Are you interested in my help?"

"Yeah, sure. Except...." He looked at my dad's suit. "I can't afford you."

"This is pro bono."

Blade seemed indifferent. So far, he had seemed that way about everything. Even when he nearly broke that guy's spine in the fabric store parking lot, he appeared to be bored.

"They've set bail at five thousand," my father said. "But you can post it immediately and leave with me. Apparently you haven't violated any laws recently."

Blade was modestly silent.

My dad raised his eyebrows. "Can you get that kind of money?"

"Sure."

"How soon?"

"A phone call."

My dad called for the sergeant and they talked about Blade making a call. While the sergeant set it up, my dad talked with Blade some more and said something about not wanting to know where he was getting the money.

"Is it in your savings account?" I said.

Blade looked at me. "Something like that, kid."

Chapter Twenty-Three

My dad was hanging up the phone in the station when he told the sergeant that a member of Blade's "motorcycle club" had dropped off the bail money in a paper bag at the court house.

"He's free to leave with you," the sergeant said and gave my dad a sheet of paper before he left the station. He seemed happier than if a freeloading relative was finally moving out.

Outside the station, my dad explained to me that the sheet was a list of priors.

"What are priors?" I said.

"Things you've done in the past."

"Oh," I said. "You mean like your baseball stats on the back of a baseball card."

"Something like that, kid," Blade said.

My dad made a slightly amused face.

There was a McDonald's just off the common. My dad made a comment about the zoning laws in the town and it seemed like he didn't think they were very good. He said to Blade that he normally would meet with a client in his Boston office, but this was an unusual case and we should expedite it.

My dad has a big vocabulary.

"I'm sure Aiden's hungry," he said. "Let's convene at McDonald's."

I thought the teenage girl at the cash register was going to resign her job when the three of us entered the restaurant. She couldn't have been more scared if we had come in holding scythes and wearing hooded black robes. My dad made her feel better when he spoke on our behalf. He also asked for a receipt, for the law firm.

My dad got coffee. Blade got three quarter pounders with cheese, two large fries and a soft drink in a cup that held about a barrel of soda. I got a hamburger and a shake.

The Ronald McDonald room at the back of the restaurant was empty, so we sat there. A sign informed us that it was available for birthday parties.

My dad read the sheet of paper that the sergeant had given him, then he looked at Blade and back at me. "I can send Aiden to the car while we discuss this," he said.

"I got no secrets."

My dad skimmed the sheet again. "Maybe you should." He read the sheet a third time and said, "Is there anything you haven't done?"

Blade shrugged and made a modest smile.

"I'm certain I can keep you out on the D and D charge."

"D and D?" I said.

Blade almost seemed embarrassed. "Drunk and disorderly. Sorry, kid."

"We don't need to go into too many details here," my father said. "Your prior history may be problematic. However, my sister is willing to speak on your behalf as a character witness."

Blade nodded. "Why are you doing this?"

"It's for my sister. It's a long story. I went into law in part because I believed in the principle of a fair hearing for everyone in a court of law."

"Even people like me?" Blade said.

"Everyone deserves a fair hearing, even if I doubt their innocence," my dad said. "Besides, I've had clients with more, um, challenging situations than yours."

"That's hard to believe," Blade said.

"They were more subtle about it."

I was thinking to myself as they talked that Blade was pretty articulate for such a scary guy.

A trio of older teenagers walked by us on the way to the bathroom. They looked away when Blade stared at them. I saw a mom with two young children at a booth and the kids were having Happy Meals. For some reason, I noticed that the Muzak was playing a cheesy version of a hit song from a few years ago.

My dad and Blade talked for about ten minutes more, with my dad taking notes as Blade spoke. My dad used a lot of legal terms. Blade seemed familiar with most of them. Practice, I guess.

Blade finished his 8,000 calorie meal before my dad got halfway through his coffee. "Did I ruin your appetite, Mr. McManus?"

My dad smiled. "No, not at all. I'll eat with my wife when I get home. You're much better company than a number of clients I've had." He shuffled his papers together and slipped them into a brown legal folder. "I think I have all the information I need. Can I drop you somewhere?"

"My bike is back at the house where…."

Before he finished, my dad said, "We'll take you there."

Chapter Twenty-Four

Bernie popped up everywhere I went in school over the next few weeks, or maybe I was just more aware of him. He was in the cafeteria at lunch. He passed my locker in the hall between classes. It was like I couldn't avoid him if I was trying to.

I noticed that I wasn't mad when I saw Bernie now. I felt sad and even embarrassed a couple of times, but I didn't feel like hurting him anymore. Maybe because he didn't seem so lucky anymore. Sure, he had survived the car accident. Sure, he had been under the influence and still lived. But his life seemed so hard to me, just walking was a challenge and so was making friends. And, this was the big thing, I had realized that Bernie had nothing to do with what happened to Jack. Jack was my best friend and it still would've hurt if Bernie had never existed. I was kind of proud of myself for finally realizing that.

"It's weird how he keeps showing up," I told Tommy one day.

"Here's your cue," Tommy said.

"What?"

Tommy pointed down the hall. Bernie was coming in our direction. Again.

At dinner, Eileen announced that Robert Erskine was giving the valedictorian address at commencement. She seemed distressed about it.

I listened because my aunt had recently told me that girls who were Eileen's age just needed you to listen without saying anything back. I was practicing now. Eileen made it easier because it was rare you could get a word in anyway.

"He's already been accepted at Oberlin for music," she said. "And he has become completely impossible."

"Oberlin is a fine college," my father said. "We could visit it this summer."

"Why would I do that?"

"Maybe you'd like to apply there."

"I want to go closer to home," Eileen said.

"Travis still hasn't heard from any colleges," I said.

"We're not talking about baseball." Eileen scowled at me.

"Are you in charge of topics?"

"Dad, do we need to talk about Aiden's baseball team right now?"

"Eileen," my dad said. "He just made a comment and it's related to college."

"We love you both the same," my aunt said.

Eileen quieted down.

"Coach made some suggestions for colleges where they had good teams," I said. "But Travis wants to go to one of the big schools. He thinks he's too good for a small college."

"He told you that?" my mother said.

"I heard him say it in the locker room, but I really think it's his dad's opinion. Travis's father won't take him to see any small ones."

My dad shook his head, just a slight bit. I could tell he didn't agree with Travis's father. I was thinking that was one of the reasons Travis had been so mean to me. It didn't make me like him more, but at least it didn't seem so personal.

"I guess we're done talking about me going to college," Eileen said.

"Dearie, that's no so." My aunt gave her a sympathetic smile. "Of course we're not done."

We spent the rest of dinner talking about Eileen and college, which made her happy. It sort of made me happy, too, seeing her feel better. I like being in my family at times like this.

Chapter Twenty-Five

It was Friday evening after dinner and I asked my parents if it was okay if I went to see Bernie. My father asked where he lived and I said I was pretty sure I knew where to find him. He offered to give me a ride, but I said I wanted to take my bike.

I got my bike from the garage and rode toward the high school. My gut told me that he would be hanging out in the woods with the other freaks. Other than riding to the woods, I didn't have much of a plan. Steve McGarrett and Mannix would've had a plan.

I got to the school and walked my bike through the staff parking lot in front. The evening was silent except for the echo of volleyed tennis balls from the courts beyond the baseball field. I looked over and could see the glare of lights from the towers at the courts. The rear wheel of my bike clicked rhythmically with my stride.

I caught a whiff of cigarette smoke when I turned the corner of the building. It had to be coming from the thicket of trees a hundred yards ahead because there were no people in sight, except for the tennis players. I figured they weren't smoking.

The thicket was an open secret at school. People knew it was where the freaks went to party. I wondered why the police just let it go. They probably had bigger issues to deal with.

I thought of my idea of a party, being at home with my family and friends, eating good stuff that my mom had made. Standing out in the woods in the dark almost made the party with Ryan attractive. I knew the grassy area between the school and the thicket well because Jack and I used to come here when we were still in elementary school to play catch and dream about playing varsity baseball. There isn't an inch of this area that's unfamiliar to me.

A break in the trees formed an opening that had been worn down by foot traffic. It resembled a hiking trail. The closer I got to the trees, the weirder I began to feel. What was the point of coming here? Why was I bothering with Bernie?

Something inside me kept my feet moving. I couldn't put it in words. It was just a gut thing. I heard voices when I got to the edge of the thicket and I stopped for a minute. *There's still time to turn around*, I thought. The smell of smoke was stronger and not just cigarette smoke. My idea suddenly seemed less great to me. Actually, it hadn't been that great to begin with.

I propped my bike against a tree near the opening, just out of sight of the field. I didn't like my idea at all anymore, but I went in anyway.

About ten or fifteen yards into the woods, there was a small clearing and I saw a group of kids sitting and standing in a circle. I didn't want them to see me right away, so I kept a tree between me and them, out of their sight line. The group was a mix of ages, ranging from a few freshmen to full-blown adults. I recognized a kid from my homeroom class who was so quiet and uninvolved with school that it was as though he wasn't even a member of the student body. A few girls, the hippie types, were in the circle. The kids here that I recognized didn't bother anyone at school. In a way, they were invisible during the school day.

I saw the senior in my wood shop who was making a beautiful end table out of mahogany. A townie from the crowd that hangs out at the supermarket parking lot was wearing a fedora, smoking a cigarette, and holding a

101

Pabst Blue Ribbon beer. It was like a juvenile version of the party I went to with Ryan.

I stepped forward along the path until I was a few yards from them.

Someone said, "What's he doing here?"

"Hey look, it's a jock," another voice said.

Everyone in the circle stopped talking and stared at me. I felt like a Martian, only weirder.

Bernie was easy enough to recognize because he was standing next to Ryan. I got now why Ryan had been acting the way he had been acting. I figured that he had found out about the party with the Mullen bothers and Blade from this crowd.

While the others stared, Bernie limped toward me. "This is it," he said.

"What?"

"What we do most nights."

"What about school and homework and that stuff?" I said.

Bernie kind of stood there without answering. "This is it. This is what we like to do."

I thought about Mr. Frazier at the bleachers and how he had said that Bernie was fulfilling the terms of his probation. It didn't look that way to me.

"Don't you think about college?" It was the first thing to come out of my mouth.

"Never," Bernie said. "We just live each day."

"Don't you ever feel like doing something else? I mean, like just breaking away?"

"I can't. This is where I belong."

"You could think about better places. Imagine it in your head first. That sort of thing."

"That positive thinking stuff never works," he said.

102

Someone tapped me on the wrist. It was a girl in an Indian headband with a feather, but she was no more Native American than me. I recognized her from the tenth graders. She handed me a joint. I shook my head. She passed it to a kid with long black hair who was wearing a military fatigue jacket with a corporal's patch, sort of like the jacket John Lennon started wearing after the Beatles broke up.

"Why'd you come?" Bernie said. He didn't seem glad or upset I was there. He didn't seem anything. Just a kid skating along the surface.

"I don't even know." I did know that I wanted to leave.

"Do you approve?"

"It's not for me to approve," I said.

"You're not like the other jocks."

I never thought of myself as a category, but I guess Bernie did. "Jocks are a pretty broad range of people."

The talking had started up again. The group seemed to have forgotten about me and Bernie, or to at least accepted that I wasn't there to bust them or something.

I felt awkward just being there. They didn't seem to have any direction. They were just killing time. At least, that's how it appeared to me, but I was an outsider looking in. Maybe they saw it differently. "Do your folks know you're here?"

"Do yours?" Bernie said caustically. It was the first real, spontaneous emotion he had shown.

"Yeah, they do."

He was surprised. "We just come here. We don't tell anyone."

My family was very different. I wouldn't want them to just let me go and never ask about it. I overheard someone say they had done Quaaludes the previous night. If I needed a cue to leave, that was it.

"After the bleachers that Saturday," I said. "I thought I'd try."

"Try what?"

"Nothing. I'm gonna head home. I wanted you to know that there were no hard feelings. See you around, I guess."

Bernie didn't say goodbye or even acknowledge me leave. He returned to the circle and the others.

I wondered if Bernie cared at all that I had tried, but I wasn't really doing it for him in the first place.

I walked toward the opening where I'd left my bike, thinking it had been a colossal mistake to come. I should've known how it would've been. I couldn't imagine what I was thinking when I came up with the idea to visit Bernie and the other freaks.

I found my bike and was shaking my head when a bright light shone in my face. It blinded me and I put my hands in front of my face to shield my eyes.

"Stop right there," an adult voice said. "Police."

The light went from my face to my feet. Two cops were standing there. I couldn't make out who they were because I was still seeing spots from the light.

"That's Aiden McManus."

"What?" the other cop said. "What's he doing here?"

"Well?" the first cop said.

"It's a long story and a stupid idea of mine," I said.

"Try us."

I heard the snap of twigs and brush and the rush of feet behind me. The noise was moving in the opposite direction of where I was standing.

"They're getting away," a tall, younger cop said.

"That's okay. We were just trying to roust them," an older, heavy cop said.

I recognized both cops now. It's a small police force for a small town.

"Do you smell that? Pot." The younger cop looked at the older one.

"Your coach know you're here?" the older cop said.

"No, but my parents do." I then explained to them about the social worker's visit to our house and the meeting on the bleachers with Mr. Frazier and how they thought it would be a good idea for me to get to know Bernie better.

"Social workers got strange ideas. I say just leave well enough alone." The older cop put his flashlight back in his utility belt. "Let's call in." He looked at me. "Go home. This is no place for a kid playing varsity baseball."

The cops returned to the squad car in the parking lot and I walked my bike across the open field to the other side of the high school. I mounted my bike when I got to the service road and pedaled home.

Chapter Twenty-Six

Aunt Lindy was drinking tea at the kitchen table and reading the *Globe* when I got home. There was a TableTalk pie next to the newspaper. I hadn't considered it before, but being retired, living with your favorite brother, and eating pie was a pretty good way to spend your time.

"Did you find him?" she said.

I nodded. "Yeah."

"They smoke. I can smell it."

I nodded again.

"Get changed and put your clothes in the hamper. We'll get them cleaned up." She put her hand over mine and squeezed it gently. "You did a lovely thing."

"I didn't do anything." I described for her the kids hanging around with nothing to do but drink and get high. At least, that's all they figured they could do. I told her how Bernie had never given college or anything beyond high school a thought and was just killing time. In my opinion, anyhow. I didn't mention the police.

"They sound sad to me," my aunt said.

"I guess so."

"A lot of people are sad."

"How do you know?"

"I've been around a long time," my aunt said. "Check in with your father and mother before you go to bed. They're upstairs."

"Sure, Aunt Lindy."

She squeezed my hand again.

"I'm glad you live with us, Aunt Lindy," I said.

"Me too. Good night."

I went to my parents' room. My dad was sitting in a chair and reading. My mom was putting clothes away in the closet. I told them about the woods and seeing Bernie.

"Makes it a little harder to keep hating him," my dad said.

"I don't hate him."

"Did it help?" my mom said.

"What? Going there? I don't know. It made everything more complicated."

"Bernie's been an easy target." she said.

"Do you think I've treated Bernie badly?"

"Yeah, I do. I'm not blaming you, but I do. So what's next?"

"I guess I could just let him be," I said. "Let him go his way. I never thought the meeting with him was much of a good idea, anyway. We don't need to be buddies, you know. Just let him be. I think that's what Jack would want me to do."

What people didn't understand was that I didn't hate Bernie. It might have sounded like I did, but I didn't really. Hate takes a lot of energy and I simply didn't have it in me to keep churning inside. Maybe it was getting suspended from the team and missing baseball or seeing how screwed up your life can get if you let it. Bernie. Harold. The townies in the bus depot. I was pretty lucky, the way I saw it. My dad was right, I figured, about how people can really make a mess of things and then they need a lawyer or someone to help them clean it up.

I felt sorry for Bernie now, and not in a I'm-better-than-you kind of way. He had a life I didn't want. Hating him would be piling on after life had already pinned him.

Chapter Twenty-Seven

On the evening of commencement, Tommy and I walked to the football field. Everyone else had the same idea about arriving early because all the seats in the bleachers were taken or reserved. Townies, college students home for the summer, young and old residents were all in the crowd. It seemed as if the whole town had turned out for the ceremony.

When Jack and I were in elementary school, we used to play touch football off to the side of the track during the ceremony. No one seemed to mind because we were just dumb kids. I really liked those times. They were some of the best memories I had.

Now that it was high school, I figured I should listen to the speakers and watch the diplomas get handed out. Besides, a couple of my teammates were graduating.

"It's almost eighty degrees," I said as we looked around for kids we knew.

"It feels like August," Tommy said.

"It looks like everyone who ever went to school here is back."

"Even the ones who cut class every chance they got," Tommy said and nodded toward the gathering of hoods in black leather jackets in the end zone.

The hoods stood under a halo of cigarette smoke. The older brother of a kid I knew was leaning on crutches and laughing. His right leg below the knee was gone, left in Vietnam when he stepped on a landmine. I wondered how he could be so cheerful, just talking with friends, but I guess that's one of the times when everyone feels happy.

The ceremony was kind of boring and we spent most of it pushing through the crowd, trying to find people we knew. I stopped to listen when Robert Erskine was announced to give the valedictorian address. I was sort of interested in what he had to say and why he got under my sister's skin so much. He didn't have much to say, just work hard and plan for the future. The sort of thing your teachers tell you to do. It wasn't very original, but I guess it's not fair to expect a high school senior to be Solomon.

Next, they announced each senior by name and they walked up to the podium to get a diploma from the school superintendent. I saw the kid from my wood shop who had made an amazing end table, good enough that it could have been sold in a furniture store.

I wondered if Bernie was present because it was supposed to be his senior class. I wondered what he was thinking. I don't know why because I didn't like him all that much.

When the ceremony ended, a human wave pushed to the exit gates for the parking lot.

I saw Mr. Hentz ahead of us in the mass of people and he towered above most everyone in the crowd, except for the kid who graduated a couple of years ago and now was playing center at Syracuse.

"Mr. Hentz!" Tommy said it so loud that it was a little embarrassing.

A few adults looked back at us. I gave Tommy a stern look so that they wouldn't think it was me.

Mr. Hentz stopped and waved for us to come over. The crowd moved around him. No one pushed him along. He was just as commanding here as in the classroom.

"Aiden, Tommy. I'd like you to meet my wife."

Mr. Hentz's wife was pretty and had a real strong posture that made me think she might have been an athlete in college.

"These are a couple of my best students," Mr. Hentz said.

She smiled at us.

"Aiden." Mr. Hentz stopped there. He seemed to have forgotten what to say or wasn't sure if he should say whatever was on his mind. Then he looked at Tommy. "I'm sure you two will make good choices tonight."

"We're just going home, Mr. Hentz," Tommy said. "There are some parties, but we're going to skip them. Probably just be a lot of drinking and stuff."

"Sounds like a wise choice." Mr. Hentz glanced at his wife.

She raised her eyebrows as if she knew my story already. I sensed that she knew more than she was letting on. That was okay, though it felt a little strange that someone I had never met before knew about my life. "I remember high school like it was yesterday."

"Did you like it?" Tommy said.

"Yes," she said. "Very much." She made an expression like a lot of good things must have happened when she was our age. "I guess you young men should be off now."

We said our goodbyes to Mr. Hentz and his wife and Tommy and I blended into the crowd. I was about to say something to Tommy when I heard my name shouted from off in the distance. I looked around, wondering where the voice had come from.

"Aiden!" I heard again.

Tommy traced the voice to the visitor's bleachers. On the other side of the track, next to the bleachers.

110

Eddie Thompson had his right arm in the air, waving at us. He was still wearing this mortarboard and his graduation gown was flapping all around him.

Tommy and I changed our route, left the crowd, and walked toward Eddie.

"Didn't expect to see you here," he said.

"We wanted to support our teammates," I said.

Tommy scanned the crowd. "Did Travis show up?"

Travis hadn't earned enough credits to graduate because he had failed a science and math course. It wasn't like he wasn't able to do the work. He just didn't try. I think he was getting back at his dad, in a way, because he missed out on applying to the colleges that his father had picked out for him.

"I think he wanted to come," Eddie said. "Even though he's not getting a diploma, you know. I think his dad grounded him."

We walked up the small hill along with a stream of people moving toward the parking lot.

"He's going to summer school, I heard," Eddie said after we'd made it onto the asphalt. "He'll be able to graduate in August. They have a special ceremony, not a big one like this."

As hard a time as Travis had given me and Jack, I was sort of sad for him. "Is he going to college?"

"A couple nearby. Maybe. Close to home. Berkshire State and a couple of other schools like that," Eddie said. "Ones with baseball programs. It's not like he's gonna play pro or anything. To think he was going to play for the Red Sox was always a fantasy. Especially for his dad."

"I think every kid who plays baseball around here has that same fantasy," Tommy said.

Eddie glanced back at the high school. "What are you doing for the summer?"

"Tommy and I are playing baseball for the town," I tried to say indifferently. I felt a little weird because Tommy and I would still be playing for the town and Eddie's days of doing that were over. He was going on to college, which was great, but he wasn't going to play baseball. It was a Division One school and strictly scholarship players.

"You have a chance to go to a good college with a big-time baseball program, you know," Eddie said. "With your talent."

"I guess so," I said, though I wasn't sure if I still felt the same way about it as when Jack was alive.

"Well, I gotta go," Eddie said.

Eddie melted into the crowd and Tommy and I walked away from the football field to the open space just beyond the school. It was the quickest way to get back to the center, especially if you're on foot.

In the distance, I could see the opening in the thicket and I wondered if the freaks were in there tonight. With the bigger police presence on account of commencement, I thought they might not be, but, then again, they probably didn't much care about the police, or anything else.

My curiosity got the better of me. "I need to check something."

"What?"

"There." I pointed to the woods and the opening for the trail.

"What do you want with that?" Tommy said. "That's the freaks' spot."

"I know," I said. "But I need to know something."

112

We cut diagonally across the field toward the thicket. I didn't hesitate this time when we got to the trail opening, probably because Tommy was with me and probably because I'd been here before. Our sneakers cracked twigs and leaves beneath them, giving ample warning to anyone who was in there.

"Everyone is probably doing the usual thing," I said and I quickly explained to Tommy what had happened the last time I was in the thicket.

"It's better being out in the open air," Tommy said.

"Matter of opinion." I saw a circle of teenagers, the usual ones from school, and a few older freaks who were not quite townies because they didn't hang out in the shopping center parking lot. I wondered what they did all day long. At least the townies had jobs at the gas station or the dairy or driving trucks for stores.

They were smoking and drinking, which was no surprise, and Bernie was among them, which was no surprise, either.

Tommy didn't seem to know what to say. He had this expression that he had just entered some exotic place that he wanted to leave.

"It's that jock," I heard someone say.

"He brought another one with him," someone else said, as if we were a circus act.

Bernie looked at me without acknowledgement, like I was some stranger. He put a joint to his lips, pulled on it, held his breath, and let out a long exhale of white smoke.

"Why did we come here?" Tommy said in a low voice. He was as uncomfortable as I'd been the first time I came to the thicket.

"I wanted to see someone."

"Who?"

"Turned out to be nobody. Sorry." I turned around and walked out to the open field with Tommy.

Outside in the open, Tommy said, "Who were you looking for?"

"Bernie Kimball."

Tommy screwed up his face. "What for?"

"I don't actually know at this point." I didn't know. My mind was a blank for a moment. "I guess I wanted to see what he was doing on his graduation night. At least the night that was supposed to be his."

"I guess it makes sense to you," Tommy said.

I was about to explain to him the meeting on the football bleachers with Bernie and Mr. Frazier and Ms. Friedkin, but it seemed a waste of time. Things were the way they were and they weren't going to change. At least not for Bernie any time soon, it appeared.

We took the service road and cut across the playground at the elementary school. We went past the swings and the monkey bars where Jack and I had spent hundreds of recess periods. We reached the common in the center of town and I could almost feel the warmth of my mother's and aunt's voices when I got home.

At the intersection in the center where Jack had been killed, Tommy and I stopped and waited for the walk light.

The light changed. Tommy started across. I stayed there. My feet wouldn't move. Halfway across the street, Tommy stopped and gave me a puzzled look. The walk light started to flash orange and Tommy had to get out of the road because a big, long line of cars coming from the high school was waiting for the light to change.

I cupped my hands around my mouth and shouted to him. "Next light!"

Tommy jogged back to my side of the street. As he did, a car on the far side of the intersection tried to make a quick left turn against the traffic as soon as the light went green. It was a bonehead move.

The brakes screeched from a car coming in the opposite direction, followed by a loud crunching sound. The car slammed into the right front fender of the bonehead who had tried to make the turn. The car's radiator was now spewing steam into the night sky. The two drivers got out of their cars and stood in the middle of the intersection, cursing at each other. The drivers in the cars waiting to move leaned on their horns.

"It was a matter of inches," I said to Tommy.

"What was?" He was having trouble hearing me in the din.

"Between making it through the intersection or not." I pointed at the car with the crushed fender. "That dope's lucky nobody got hurt."

Tommy shrugged and said, "Yeah, I guess he is."

"It doesn't make sense."

"What doesn't?" Tommy said.

"The stuff people do," I said. "They don't think about how they affect everyone else."

"Be nice if they did."

I nodded as Tommy said it, but I knew it was a fantasy, like thinking Jack should have gotten a fairer shot at life, or that people change when you want them to, or believing in Bruno.

© 2018 Michael Herlihy

ABOUT THE AUTHOR

Michael Herlihy is a writer living in Bethesda, Maryland.

Made in United States
North Haven, CT
26 October 2021